Elf Road

Also by Jacqui Hazell

For Children
Horace Fox in the City

By Jaq Hazell

For Young Adults
My Life as a Bench

For Adults
I Came to Find a Girl
London Tsunami & other Stories

Elf Road

JACQUI HAZELL

Nowness Books

ISBN: 978-0-9957268-6-4

Edited by Monica Byles
Cover design by Jacqui Hazell

A CIP catalogue record for this book is available from the British
Library

For Sergio, Margot and Franky

Chapter One

Near the bottom left-hand corner of England in the Cornish village of Mousehole, halfway along Duck Street, sits a row of fishermen's cottages and at the end of that row is Stargazy Cottage. If you go round the back of Stargazy Cottage at lunchtime, you may well see two small faces peering out of the window. Tizzy Biff, aged nine, and her little brother Wilf – cat-watching.

Most days are much the same as they look out to count the cats that follow their dad home from work, and so it was, one chilly day last December.

'I can see five.' Tizzy pointed out two black cats, a pair of tabbies and a ginger.

Wilf scanned their small terraced garden looking for more furry friends. 'There's one! That makes six.' Wilf only liked even numbers.

'Those cats love my cooking.' Dad removed a giant steaming pie from the oven and the smell of fish filled the kitchen and beyond.

This wasn't just any old meal – Dad had made a stargazy pie, a local dish with fish heads poking out of the pastry as if they were having one last look at the stars up above.

Dad always practised this dish before the local pie contest. This takes place on Tom Bawcock's Eve, right before Christmas – a magical time in Mousehole with lights in the harbour, a lantern parade and the famous contest. It's all to celebrate a fisherman called Tom Bawcock who is said to have lived hundreds of years ago in the village. The story goes that he once went out to sea in a bad storm and caught enough fish to feed everyone, saving them all from starvation.

'I love stargazy pie.' Tizzy looked dreamily at the golden-brown crust oozing with sauce at the edges, and the fish poking through looked solemnly back at her. 'It means it's nearly Christmas.'

Outside, the cats paced up and down, licking their lips.

Singing an old ditty, Dad took a slice of pie through to Mum, who was sitting cosy by the fire.

Tizzy and Wilf sat up at the table. While they ate, they watched the cats, and the cats watched Tizzy and Wilf. And as soon as they'd finished, Tizzy cleared the plates, saving any leftovers, and Wilf ran outside to shoo away the seagulls.

'Pilchards!' Tizzy threw down the scraps and the cats pounced.

'The gulls didn't get a look-in.' Dad laughed.

'Oh no, five birds – odd number.' Wilf waved his arms and ran at them.

'You've scoffed the lot, you clever kitties.' Tizzy showed the empty plate and after checking for any last tasty bits, the cats slunk away down the side alley to the next cottage while the gulls shrieked in complaint.

Back indoors, it was warm and toasty by the fire, but Mum was huddled in an armchair with a blanket.

'How are you feeling?' Tizzy asked. 'Can I get you anything?'

'Just a little tired, love – nothing to worry about.'

But Tizzy did worry, because Mum had been ill for quite some time and even though the doctors were doing their best, Mum was weak and often sleepy.

Tizzy fetched her a glass of water and Wilf found Mum's favourite pillow.

'Thank you, my ducklings, but that's enough fussing.' Mum gave Wilf a squeeze. 'Your dad's going to take you over to Bib and Bob's while I have a rest.'

Dad checked Mum had everything she needed while Tizzy helped Wilf on with his coat.

'Wear a hat,' Tizzy said, 'then we won't have to brush our hair.'

Chapter Two

The Biffs only ever went to Bib and Bob's Toyshop for birthdays and Christmas, so a trip there was always a special occasion.

It was snowing when they arrived, and the wonky building that was Bib and Bob's was lit up like a fairground ride.

Wilf pressed his nose to the glass. 'Four boats, six dinosaurs, two cars and two puppets.' He counted the toys displayed in the window and nodded his approval.

'Ah, even numbers – it's almost as if they knew you were coming.' Dad pushed open the door and they felt a rush of welcome warmth as they entered the squish and squash of a shop that was piled high with all the latest toys.

Taking the first aisle, Tizzy craned her neck to inspect every shelf. 'Look at all this – how will I ever choose?'

The towering figure of Bob stood at the till serving a short lady in a mint-green coat.

'Well, hello to the Biffs!' Bob had a deep bellowing voice with the local Cornish burr. 'Fantastic fish today, as always.' He shook Dad's hand.

'Did your cat have some?' Tizzy asked.

'Oh yes, Bib was purring. I've never seen a happier cat. Now, how can I help the Biffs today?'

* * *

'We're looking for ideas,' Tizzy said.

'Pesky things, ideas,' Bob said. 'I find they turn up when you least expect it. Going for a long walk works for me. I have my most brilliant and some might say barmy ideas when I reach a brisk and steady pace.'

'Well, we walked to get here,' Wilf said.

'And we'll walk around your shop,' Tizzy added. 'The trouble is, we need to write to Father Christmas quite soon.'

'You'll write today,' Dad insisted. 'Best not to put off what you can do today, because who knows what tomorrow will bring.'

Bob stroked his stubbly chin. 'Christmas is coming and Santa needs to know what he needs to know. You're on an important mission. Christmas gift ideas are essential, time-sensitive information. Everyone needs ideas and those ideas need to be the right ones.'

Dad nodded. 'It's so much better to see these toys in the real world.'

'Exactly,' Bob agreed. 'I heard of a girl who asked for a teddy bear she'd seen online. She expected a proper cuddly bear, but when it turned up, it was the teeniest tiny thing, no bigger than the palm of my hand.'

Tizzy was confused by this, because Bob's hand looked big to her.

Dad, who was small and skinny in comparison, said, 'That's why we're here. Tizzy and Wilf need to take a good look at all the toys and choose one or two things they really want.'

'Well, you're in luck. This very morning, well before any of you young whippersnappers were awake, I received a delivery direct from Ootah.'

'Ootah, where's Ootah?' Tizzy asked.

'Did I say Ootah? Oh, silly me. It's the elves, my dear. Santa's elves have sent me samples direct from their workshop at Santa's grotto. Bib and Bob's has a large selection of the toys they're making this year, so take a good look around.'

Tizzy spotted Buzzkidz, the games console she'd seen on TV. It looked amazing, with loads of games and brilliant graphics. *Maybe that's what I'll ask for*, she thought.

Wilf, meanwhile, was rearranging the toy boats into groups of even numbers.

'Santa must get more letters than anyone else in the whole wide world.' Tizzy rolled her eyes as she imagined a mountain of letters. 'I don't know how he manages to read them all.'

'It's a challenge and, like me, Santa needs glasses.' Bob felt around the counter until he located his specs on top of his head.

'Does he like getting so many letters?' Tizzy asked.

Wilf made a face. 'Everyone likes letters.'

'I used to love getting letters when I was a kid,' Dad said, 'but now I only receive bills. No one likes bills, and I suppose all the letters to Santa are asking for something too, so they're a bit like bills.'

'Bills, bills, bills!' Bob sang like an opera singer. 'We all hate bills.'

'You think Father Christmas hates letters?' Tizzy's mouth fell open.

'This is getting a little out of hand.' Bob signalled for

everyone to calm down. 'I know for sure that it's fine to write one letter a year to Santa. It's a big help to the great man, so long as you only ask for what you really want. It's best to leave Santa some room for surprises.'

Tizzy wondered how Father Christmas coped at his busiest time of year. 'Maybe Santa just knows what everyone wants and that's how he manages to go all around the world in one single night.'

Bob scratched his head. 'The thing is, the great man whizzes around the globe with ease because children tell him where they live and what they really, really want.'

'The great man – you mean Father Christmas?' Wilf asked.

'That's him, the one and only. Some call him Santa or Santa Claus and others say Father Christmas. Whatever you like, he's the big guy in red who handles all requests. Now, take a good look and make sure you don't miss a thing: cars and boats are there, dolls and teddy bears are that way, and then we have skateboards and computer games, footballs and action figures. The elves have done an amazing job. There's so much variety. Take your time and choose your favourite toys and when you get home, write those important letters and send them to Santa at you know where.'

'You tell us the address every year,' Wilf said.

'I wouldn't want you to send your letters to the wrong place,' Bob said.

Picturing Santa's snow-capped log cabin, Tizzy smiled and said, 'It's 123 Elf Road, North Pole.'

Chapter Three

It is 2,756 miles from Cornwall to the North Pole.

Tizzy looked it up as soon as she got home.

'You'd better hurry and write those letters to Santa,' Dad said. 'They have a long way to travel, so let's get them done and we'll catch the last post.'

Wilf lined up his boats in pairs along the table.

'Why are you drawing a boat?' Tizzy asked.

'It's the broken one. I'm showing Santa what it's like.'

'You want the same thing again?'

Wilf nodded. 'I need two the same. And mother and baby giraffes.'

Mum looked over and shrugged.

As soon as they'd finished writing their letters, Dad, Tizzy and Wilf trudged through the snow to the red postbox at the end of Duck Street.

Tizzy made a wish as she pushed her letter through the slot. Closing her eyes, she imagined it taking flight all the way to the North Pole, where a kindly postwoman was waiting at the sorting office. She would collect Tizzy's letter and take it that last mile or so to a lovely little log cabin festooned with fairy lights at 123 Elf Road.

'Listen, you two, there's something I need to talk to you about,' Dad said, interrupting Tizzy's daydream. He crouched down to Tizzy and Wilf's height and put an arm around each of them. 'There's nothing to worry about, but your mum has to go into hospital for some special treatment and we don't know how long for.'

'Mum's going to be all right, isn't she?' Tizzy felt her heart thumping inside.

'She's getting the best possible care.'

'But why does she have to stay in hospital?' Wilf asked. 'We'll look after her.'

'It's easier for the doctors if she's in hospital. They have all their special equipment to hand and they can check on her all the time.'

Tizzy thought about what she could do to help. 'I can look after Wilf while you're at work,' she said. 'I'll make soup and toast and beans.'

Dad gave a sad smile. 'I'm afraid you're both too young to be left on your own. Your grandmother, Gloriana, is going to look after you in London.'

'But we don't know her!' Wilf gasped. 'We've never met her. We don't even know what she looks like.'

'This is your chance to get to know each other. It's all arranged.'

Tizzy frowned. 'But you said she's not that nice?'

'She'll be nice to you.'

'I'm not going.' Wilf folded his arms.

'I'm sorry but there's no choice. I can't look after you. I have to work.'

'Can't you take time off while Mum's ill?' Tizzy asked.

'It's not that simple,' Dad said. 'Your mum can't do her teaching right now, so I have to put in extra hours to pay the bills.'

'Bills, I hate bills!' Tizzy said.

'How long will we have to stay in London?' Wilf asked.

'It's hard to say. It depends on how the treatment goes. Try to look on the bright side – there's so much to see and do in London. Think of it as an adventure.'

'We don't want an adventure,' Tizzy said. 'We want to stay and help Mum.'

'You'll be helping Mum by going away for a while,' Dad explained. 'It's the best and most helpful thing you can do.'

Heavy snow was settling on the postbox, the garden walls and the pavement. Duck Street had never looked prettier and it hurt to think of leaving Mousehole, but Tizzy knew she had to help Mum and if that meant going away for a while, then that was what she'd do. 'When do we have to go?' she asked.

'Tomorrow morning. The train tickets are already booked.'

'Will we be home by Christmas? I'd hate to miss Tom Bawcock's Eve.' Tizzy loved the lights, the lanterns and the pie contest.

Dad took a deep breath. 'Like I said, it's hard to say how long you'll be away.'

With their heads down, Tizzy and Wilf kicked at the snow as they made their way back home to Stargazy Cottage.

In the morning, the cats gathered in the garden as usual.

Mum had tears in her eyes. 'My ducklings are leaving Duck Street,' she said.

They hugged each other tight and didn't want to let go.

Goodbye Mum, goodbye cats, and goodbye Stargazy Cottage.

Tizzy drew a sad face on the inside of the window as Dad started the car to drive away from their little white cottage, the only home she and Wilf had ever known.

'You'll love London.' Dad had only good things to say as he drove them to the station in Penzance. 'The Cornwall to London train line is the best ride ever. Wait till you see how close to the sea the tracks are at Dawlish. You'll see loads of boats, Wilf. And remember, Granny Gloriana will be there waiting for you at the other end. Look for the lady in the red coat and hat.'

Tizzy repeated what her dad had said at Bib and Bob's: 'Who knows what tomorrow will bring?'

Chapter Four

There was no way Tizzy would cry, not in public, on a train, and especially not in front of the ticket inspector who was staring down at her through thick-lensed glasses.

'I repeat, where is your mother?' His nostrils flared as he glared at Tizzy.

The carriage was quiet and people were listening and Tizzy didn't want to answer out loud, because that would make it real and she didn't want it to be real.

'Well?'

With an icy glare back and through gritted teeth, Tizzy said, 'My mum's in hospital.'

The inspector made a face like he didn't believe her. 'Are you travelling alone?'

'No,' she said, which was true because Wilf was beside her, pushed forward in his seat by his backpack, which he refused to take off.

'How old are you?' the inspector asked. 'Have you run away from home?'

Blinking back tears, Tizzy thought of Mum and Dad and Stargazy Cottage, the cats that would be waiting to be fed, and who on earth would run away just before Christmas? 'We'd never do that,' she said.

'Minors can't travel alone. You're too young.'

'They're with me.' A white-haired lady seated opposite scowled at the inspector and said, 'I'm their Great-Aunt Iris.'

The inspector studied Tizzy and Wilf's tickets and then fixed his boggle-eyed stare on Iris. 'Tell me, where are you all going?' he said, testing her to see if she knew.

Iris gave him the sweetest smile and shook her white head. 'My memory's gone. That's why they're with me. They're such a great help.'

'You don't even know their names, do you?'

Iris's twinkly eyes crinkled a little more at the edges. 'I do know. Their names are locked forever here inside, close to my heart.' She tapped her chest.

The inspector looked back at Tizzy. 'I want to speak to your parents. Call them on your phone.'

'I don't have a phone.'

'All kids have mobile phones these days.'

'We don't,' Tizzy said.

'I think they're quite expensive,' Wilf said.

Iris nodded. 'We all get on perfectly fine without those noisy things.'

The train slowed as it approached its next stop beside the sea at Dawlish.

Wilf edged closer to the window to look at the boats anchored offshore. 'That one is a Hardy Mariner and that's a Bluewater yacht.'

'Bit of an expert on boats, are we?' The inspector handed back their tickets. 'I'll be checking on you again.' He shook his head and moved on to the next carriage.

Tizzy breathed out. 'Thank you so much.' She smiled at Iris.

'I'm sorry to hear your mother is unwell.'

'We have to stay with our grandma in London,' Wilf said.

'That's nice. How long are you going to be staying?'

Tizzy sighed. 'We don't know and it's nearly Christmas.

Father Christmas won't know where we are.'

'We can write to him again,' Wilf suggested.

'But didn't Bob say you should only write once a year?' Tizzy said.

'Don't worry, your grandma will let him know where you are,' Iris said.

Wilf shrugged. 'We don't know what she's like. She never visits.'

'She hates the countryside,' Tizzy added.

'Have you never visited your grandma in London?' Iris asked.

'I don't think we've been invited,' Tizzy said.

'Well, at least you're going to meet her now. It's exciting. London is wonderful at this time of year. You'll be able to see the Christmas lights.'

'We have Christmas lights in Mousehole,' Wilf said.

'And there's a lantern parade, with stargazy pie,' Tizzy added. 'It's our favourite time of year. It's two days before Christmas on Tom Bawcock's Eve, which is named after a fisherman who went out in a big storm and caught enough fish to feed the whole village. We never miss it.'

Homesick before they'd even arrived, Tizzy and Wilf looked at one another and sighed.

Five hours and thirty-four minutes later their train pulled in to Paddington Station.

Wilf, backpack firmly in place, was ready to disembark, while Tizzy helped Iris with her case.

'Thank you, dear,' Iris said. 'I'll wait with you until you find your gran.'

They sat down on a bench and looked up and down the platform, searching for a little old lady in red.

Half an hour passed.

Tizzy wished she did have a phone so she could call Dad

and check that Grandma Gloriana was on her way.

'Maybe she's forgotten,' Wilf said.

'Perhaps she's ill,' Tizzy said.

'It's probably the traffic,' Iris suggested. 'London is so busy.'

A moment later a tall thin lady in a long dark red puffer coat, wide felt hat, and chunky red boots shouted, 'You there on the bench – Tizzy and Wilf Biff, is that you?'

'Is that her?' Wilf stared at the red figure heading towards them.

Iris adjusted her glasses. 'Good heavens!'

Tizzy's mouth fell open. 'She's like a film star.'

'More like a red maggot in that padded coat.' Wilf thought she looked weird.

'It must be London fashion,' Tizzy said.

'Help me up, dears,' Iris said, and Tizzy and Wilf lent her an arm each to ease her back to her feet. 'Hello there, are you their grandma?'

The woman in red froze and her mouth went twisty.

Tizzy studied her face, confused by its smoothness. She didn't look old enough to be a grandma, and yet at the same time, she didn't look young.

'Grandma Gloriana?' Tizzy asked.

'*Grandma?* Did you say *grandma*? Never say *grandma*! That word is for *old crinkly* people.' She glanced at Iris. 'No offence, lady, but I cannot bear that word. Call me Gloriana. I have been Gloriana all my life and Gloriana I shall remain.' She looked the children up and down, reaching out to inspect Tizzy's shoulder-length brown hair. 'Rats' tails!' she exclaimed. 'We'll have to do something about that hair. And the clothes?' Tizzy was wearing her parka, jeans and trainers, as was Wilf, along with his favourite nautical sweatshirt. 'How drab,' Gloriana said, 'drab and dreary. Honestly, has no one heard of fashion in Cornwall?'

'She's so rude,' Wilf whispered.

'Sometimes the truth hurts, shorty,' Gloriana said. 'Trust

me when I say, one must be cruel to be kind.'

'May we have a drink?' Wilf asked.

'Say "please",' Tizzy whispered.

'Please,' he added.

'I have a perfectly good tap at home so you can wait until we get back there.'

'I must say you have lovely grandchildren,' Iris said. 'They looked after me the whole way here.'

'How nice for you.' Gloriana turned on her heel. 'Let's go, small fry. I have places to go and people to see.'

Tizzy turned and thanked Iris for her help.

Clasping Tizzy's hand, Iris said, 'I do hope your mother gets better soon, and don't you worry – I know Father Christmas will find you wherever you are.'

'Gloriana's nearly gone,' Wilf said. 'We'd better hurry.'

They wished Iris a happy Christmas and ran, Wilf-with-backpack and Tizzy trailing her case on wheels as they tried to catch up with the flash of dark red that was fast disappearing towards the station exit.

Chapter Five

Ashburn House, a tall building painted in a fashionable shade of dove grey, sat on a fashionable street in a fashionable part of London.

Before Gloriana opened the glossy canary yellow front door, she paused and looked down at Tizzy and Wilf. 'This is

Elbert Crescent,' she said. 'It's a smart address for smart people. Do not let me down.'

There was yapping and Gloriana opened the door to two little black dogs who jumped up high to greet them.

'I love pugs.' Tizzy stroked the small stubby dogs.

'I am so pleased because it'll now be your job to clean up after them.' Gloriana handed them each a roll of poop bags.

'They're not house-trained?' Tizzy asked.

'All dogs make the odd mistake. What you must do is clean up after my darling pooches and pop the poop in the bin down the road when you walk them twice a day, every day.'

Wilf frowned as he looked up at the sweeping staircase coiling up from the hall, and peered into the rooms running off it.

'Have you noticed anything weird?' he whispered.

Tizzy shrugged. This house was certainly far grander than their cosy, cluttered cottage in Cornwall, but she didn't think it weird exactly.

'There are no decorations,' Wilf said. 'Not even a Christmas tree!'

Tizzy's mouth fell open. 'That *is* weird,' she said.

'I don't celebrate Christmas.' Gloriana gave Wilf a sharp look, and his face crumpled. 'Pull yourself together, little man, I'm joking. The tree goes up on Christmas Eve and not a moment before. It's bad taste to decorate any earlier than that. Right, this way.' She led them through to a shiny white kitchen that reminded Tizzy of the dentist's surgery they were forced to visit every six months. Gloriana pointed to a shelf. 'The glasses are there and the tap is over the sink.'

Tizzy reached up to help.

Wilf glugged down a glassful of water. 'Nothing better when you're thirsty,' he said, 'though it tastes different here in London.'

'Right, follow me.' Gloriana took them up to the smallest room on the top floor. Painted a shabby shade of elephant-grey, it had twin beds and a window that looked out over rooftops towards a park.

'This room must be kept tidy at all times,' Gloriana ordered.

Tizzy thought that would be easy, seeing as there were only the two beds and a cupboard.

The doorbell chimed, the dogs barked and Gloriana's face lit up as if she were expecting Father Christmas himself.

'That'll be the Blings!' she said. 'Basil, Babette and their daughter Beatrice live next door. Smarten up. Grubby train-travelled faces must be washed and rats' tails combed to glossy tresses before you come down and say hello.'

Once Gloriana had gone, Wilf sat on the edge of one of the beds and stared at the small toy fishing boat he'd brought from home. 'I miss Mum and Dad.'

Tizzy nodded. 'And Stargazy Cottage and the cats.'

'And my toys.' Wilf looked around at the empty room.

Crossing her fingers, legs and toes, Tizzy said, 'This won't be for long. Mum will get better soon, I know she will.'

Wilf took a deep breath. 'Best not to think of home right now.'

Tizzy nodded. 'We'd better wash away those train smells she was on about.'

They splashed water on their faces and tried to comb their hair.

'What's wrong with rats' tails anyway?' Tizzy said.

'Yeah,' Wilf nodded. 'Rats are nature and I love nature.'

They headed downstairs, where they heard a strange whinnying sound coming from the living room.

Peeking around the door, they found Gloriana and the Blings in a tight huddle on an egg-yolk-yellow sofa, as if they'd formed a secret club.

'You're such a hoot, Basil!' Gloriana laughed, and there was that whinnying sound again.

'It's her – she's making that noise,' Wilf whispered.

'At least she's laughing. Maybe she's nicer when she's happy.'

A warm wind had blown in with the Blings. Gloriana's stark white living room was filled with the largest bunch of the pinkest flowers Tizzy had ever seen, while on a table sat a three-tiered cake stand stacked with colourful cakes and pastries.

The pugs were up on their stubby hind legs begging, while a golden-haired woman in a splashy blue dress was stabbing cake with a tiny fork. 'This is simply divine,' she said.

'It's a fondant fancy,' Gloriana said.

'May I have a taste?' A girl of around Tizzy's age, with long shiny brown hair and a matching pink tweed jacket and skirt, took a bite of the cake. 'Ew, it's kind of soapy.'

'Don't be rude, Beatrice,' her mother said.

The dogs finally noticed Tizzy and Wilf in the doorway and barked.

'Ah,' Gloriana said, 'here they are, the little ragamuffins.'

The Blings laughed, showing their big white teeth, and Basil came forward and shook hands with Wilf in a hand-crunching way that made Wilf wince.

'Ragamuffins?' Wilf frowned and looked down at his favourite pale blue sweatshirt.

'That sweater looks as if it has been washed a thousand times,' Gloriana said, 'and as for yours . . .' She looked down her nose at Tizzy's mustard-yellow jumper.

'You'll have to take them to Marmaduke's,' Babette said.

'The clothes at Marmaduke's are adorable,' Beatrice said. 'I have the catalogue.'

'It's the only book Beatrice will read,' Babette said.

'I've been updating my Christmas list, Mummy.'

'But you sent that off weeks ago, sweetie.'

'There are so many new beauty products. I really must write again.'

Her father, Basil, frowned. 'You're writing to Santa twice?'

Beatrice looked upwards as if trying to recall. 'Four times so far.'

Basil shook his head. 'I don't think anyone should write to Santa more than once. You'll confuse him or worse still, annoy him.'

'But, Daddy, now I'm a model I need curlers for my hair and make-up.'

'All essential,' Babette said. 'What about you two, what have you asked for?'

'I'd like a new toy fishing boat,' Wilf said, 'and mother and baby giraffes.'

Babette smiled. 'Stuffed cuddly plush giraffes, I presume. And you, Tizzy?'

Tizzy thought of her letter to Santa, in which she had asked for two things: firstly, for her mum to get well, and secondly, for a BuzzKidz Game Player.

'I didn't send one.' She felt herself redden because it was a lie, but she couldn't talk about Mum, not without crying, and she didn't want to cry in front of strangers.

'Argh!' Beatrice put her hands to her face in horror. 'You haven't written to Santa! You must write now. There's still time. Daddy can send it special delivery. Do you have the Marmaduke's catalogue, Gloriana?'

Tizzy glanced around the room but there were no bookshelves, only huge mirrors and framed photographs of Gloriana and her pugs.

'I suppose you can look online. One moment.' Gloriana left the room, and quickly returned with a shiny new laptop. She fired up the computer, found the website for Marmaduke's of Piccadilly and passed the laptop to Beatrice.

'Sit here.' Beatrice tapped the seat beside her, and Tizzy and Wilf plopped themselves down.

Babette sipped her tea, and said, 'Are you here for Christmas?'

Gloriana lowered her voice to a whisper, 'Normally I go somewhere hot, but this year as I have company I must remain here.' She arched an eyebrow as she looked at Tizzy and Wilf.

'Such a shame.' Babette twiddled her diamond rings. 'We're going on a Caribbean cruise.'

'Mummy booked the wrong one.' Beatrice scowled. 'I wanted the Beauty Pageant Cruise with daily dance-offs, but Mummy booked the family fun cruise with that kids' entertainer Billy Bonkers.'

'He's funny,' Tizzy said.

'It's too babyish,' Beatrice said.

Wilf perked up. 'What sort of ship are you going on?'

Beatrice curled her lip. 'How should I know? Aren't they all the same?'

Tizzy rolled her eyes because she knew what was coming.

Wilf took a deep breath. 'There is the mainstream cruise ship, the mega cruise ship, an ocean cruise ship, a luxury cruise ship, a small one, an adventure one, a river one, and best of all, an expedition cruise ship.'

'What's that?' Beatrice said with a yawn.

'An expedition cruise ship has been specially designed for remote destinations. An icebreaker vessel for instance can withstand Arctic conditions.'

Beatrice shrugged. 'I guess we're going on the luxury one.'

Scrolling through the online catalogue, Tizzy saw all the toys she'd seen at Bib and Bob's, plus some more lavish items and clothes so fancy she wouldn't even know where to wear them.

'Would you all like to come over to ours tomorrow?' Babette asked. 'Beatrice could restyle Tizzy's hair. She loves to practise her beauty skills.'

Gloriana sighed. 'How kind of you to ask, but I have an appointment with Dr Dushka at Marmaduke's.'

'I understand,' Babette said. 'No one can miss an appointment with Dr Dushka.'

'You're going to Marmaduke's – the best shop in the world?' Beatrice said.

'Is there a Santa's grotto?' Wilf asked.

'It has the best, most exclusive grotto,' Beatrice said. 'It's so sparkly and pretty, I almost cried when I went inside.'

Tizzy thought of her letter to Santa and how she'd asked him to help make Mum better. *Maybe if I visit the grotto at Marmaduke's, I can ask him direct?* she thought.

'I'd love to visit Marmaduke's,' Tizzy said.

Gloriana shrugged. 'I suppose you'll have to come along. I can't leave you at home alone.'

'Have you finished your letter to Santa?' Beatrice asked.

Tizzy added one more thing and then, after sealing the envelope, she passed it to Beatrice who passed it to Basil.

'Daddy, make sure this is posted today.'

'Why have you written another letter?' Wilf whispered. 'Bob said you should send only one a year.'

'I had to let Santa know we might be in London. That'll be okay, won't it?'

Wilf shrugged. 'I don't know.'

And again, Tizzy felt herself redden.

Chapter Six

Marmaduke's was the oldest, widest, reddest building on Piccadilly. Tizzy and Wilf had never seen anything like it, but then they had never been on the Tube before or seen so many shops, restaurants and theatres. London was all new to them, so it was a good job Gloriana was wearing such a bright blue coat because she didn't wait around.

'One cannot be late for Dr Dushka – hurry now!' she urged.

Tizzy and Wilf-with-backpack ran to catch up as Gloriana whirled around the revolving door into Marmaduke's department store.

'Where is she?' Tizzy stretched to see above the crowd in the grand hall.

'There, I can see her coat. You can't miss it,' Wilf said. 'It's the colour of one of those poison dart frogs in my World's Most Deadly book.'

'Well, frogs are nature and we love nature,' Tizzy said.

'Bright colours can be a warning.' Wilf made a face as he spotted the sign for Toy Kingdom. 'That's the way to Santa's Grotto.'

'Let's ask Gloriana if we can go later on.' Tizzy could see a hint of intense blue moving away in the distance.

'Do you smell that?' Wilf asked, as they raced through the

bakery section of the food hall, stacked high with breads, cakes and fondant fancies like the ones Gloriana had served.

The coat as blue as a poison dart frog continued to lead them onwards through a golden room filled with jewellery and watches and then into the beauty hall. This had silver walls and giant photographs of flawless faces, and at the far end was a black door that simply stated 'Dr Dushka'.

'She's gone in.' Tizzy rushed forward and pushed open the door.

'Can I help you?' A woman in a white coat was seated at the desk.

'We're with Mrs Biff.' Tizzy pointed to a smoked-glass door set in the wall behind her. 'We're her grandchildren.'

'She has grandchildren? That's news to me. Sit over there and wait.' She waved them over to a large orange sofa. 'I'll tell Mrs Biff you're here.'

A moment later Gloriana burst out from behind the glass

door. 'Grandmother!' she hissed. 'I *told* you not to use that word. Wait there and don't touch a thing.'

'We said "grandchildren" – you didn't ban that word,' Tizzy explained.

'Right, well, I'm banning it now, along with words such as granny, nanny and nan. Honestly, do I have to spell everything out?'

Wilf, who was sat forward on the orange sofa with his backpack firmly on, raised his hand and said in a shaky voice, 'Gloriana, I need a wee – please.'

'What? Speak up, I can't hear you.'

'Please may I go to the toilet?'

'Oh, for goodness' sake.' Gloriana rolled her eyes.

'The nearest restroom is back through the beauty hall near the escalator to Toy Kingdom,' the woman in the white jacket said.

Gloriana tutted. 'You should have gone before we left.'

'I didn't need it then.'

'Honestly,' she huffed, 'you'll just have to wait until I've finished. In the meantime, cross your legs.' She went back through to Dr Dushka.

They sat and waited and Wilf kicked his feet.

'Stop that,' Tizzy said.

'It's helping me.'

'Helping you what?'

'Stop peeing myself.'

'You need it that bad?'

Wilf looked at Tizzy in a way that made her realise that if she didn't do something quick there would be a puddle.

'How long do you think Mrs Biff's appointment will be?' Tizzy asked the woman in the white coat.

'Appointments last fifty minutes.'

'If Mrs Biff comes out early, please tell her we've gone to the toilet.' Tizzy grabbed Wilf by the hand and opened the door that led back out to the beauty hall. Dodging past several ladies in fancy outfits, they ran towards the escalator for Toy Kingdom.

Looking up from the golden hall to the toy floor, they could see colourful signs for Toy Kingdom and Santa's Grotto.

'Can we go?' Wilf pleaded.

'Not now. You need the loo, remember?' Rushing on, Tizzy followed the signs that led to the toilets. 'At last!' She opened the door to an ornate washroom with carved wooden doors to the left and marble sinks to the right.

Dashing into a cubicle, Wilf locked the door. 'Tizzy,' he called out, 'you know what I said about having a drink when you're really thirsty and how good that is? Well, having a wee when you're desperate is even better.'

When Wilf came out to wash his hands, he looked in awe at the low-lit room with its crystal lights and ornate mirrors. 'The carving on the doors is amazing. They're snow scenes. It looks like another world with a frozen sea and swirly skies.'

They studied the door of each cubicle. One showed a walrus and another a polar bear, but best of all, there was a ship.

'That's an expedition ship. This must be the Arctic.' Wilf touched the carved lines of the ship and the ice through which it was passing. 'This is the best toilet in the best shop in the world.'

'We'd better get back and wait for *Granny*,' Tizzy said.

'She'll be ages,' Wilf said. 'She's probably having a facelift.'

'Let's hope it's a mood-lift.'

Leaving the restrooms, they retraced their path.

'Can we go up there now?' Wilf pointed to the escalator carrying a steady stream of happy kids to Toy Kingdom. 'Gloriana won't know – she'll be ages.'

I need to see Santa, Tizzy thought. *He can help Mum.* She checked her watch. 'We can have a quick look.'

They took the escalator up and followed the signs and as soon as they entered Toy Kingdom, they were hit by a wall of colour with toys stacked to the ceiling on all sides. There was noise and laughter with shop assistants in bright red suits demonstrating different toys.

'This way for Santa's Grotto'

Tizzy and Wilf read the sign and without discussion, followed the arrows. Soon there was a buzz in the air and fairy lights. Families were waiting and there was excited chatter and Christmas music playing 'It's the Most Wonderful Time of the Year'.

I must see Santa, Tizzy thought. *He needs to know about Mum.*

They joined the end of the queue behind a mother and daughter. The mum squeezed her daughter's hand and Tizzy got a lump in her throat and had to look away.

The queue moved quickly and Tizzy and Wilf soon arrived at the entrance, where a young woman dressed as an elf was seated on a tall stool. Tizzy stared. She was fascinated by the woman's costume and red lipstick.

'Hello, and welcome to Santa's Grotto at Marmaduke's of Piccadilly. Do you have your tickets ready?'

Tizzy and Wilf looked at each other and gulped.

'We didn't know you had to book,' Tizzy said.

'Luckily there are a few tickets remaining for entry today. Tickets cost £25 each and are available to all our customers when they spend £2000 in Marmaduke's of Piccadilly. The ticket booth is back over there to your left.'

Tizzy wondered if this was a joke. 'Twenty-five pounds per ticket and you have to spend £2000 in Marmaduke's!'

'We've never had that much money,' Wilf said.

'I don't think our mum and dad have ever had that much money,' Tizzy added.

The young lady elf pursed her lips and said, 'Thank you for your interest in Santa's Grotto at Marmaduke's of Piccadilly. If you could just move along so the next family *with* tickets can enter? Merry Christmas.'

Standing aside, Tizzy and Wilf watched the lucky ticket holders edge forward.

'Beatrice Bling never said it was so expensive,' Tizzy said.

'Why should only rich kids meet Santa?' Wilf looked down at his old trainers and sighed. 'It's not fair.'

'I really want to talk to Santa.' Tizzy thought of Mum and how she hoped Santa might be able to help. 'Let's walk around the outside and see if we can peek in.'

The outer walls of Santa's Grotto were a dark inky blue with tiny lights sparkling like a galaxy. Walking around the side, they could find no other way in apart from the exit, which was guarded by another young woman dressed in an elf outfit.

'We're not going to get to see the crystal walkway,' Wilf said.

'Sometimes places are better in your imagination,' Tizzy said. 'Like when we posted our letters to Santa. I imagined my letter flying through the air all the way from Cornwall to the North Pole, where it got taken to this pretty little log cabin with fairy lights at 123 Elf Road. I doubt this Marmaduke's grotto is as lovely as that.'

Wilf nodded. 'I suppose we'd better go and wait for *Granny*.'

Tizzy grinned. 'Do you think our *gran* is missing us?'

'No, I reckon our *grandma* is glad we're out of the way.'

'I feel like saying *grandma* all the time,' Tizzy joked.

'*Granny, granny, granny!*'

They said it together and the more they said 'granny', 'gran', or 'grandma', they couldn't stop laughing, until their eyes went blurry and they couldn't see a thing.

'I'm so sorry!' Tizzy bumped into a man as he came out of a hidden side door.

The man, who was dressed in denim overalls, steadied himself. 'No worries, miss, I wasn't looking myself.'

'Did you come from the grotto?' Tizzy asked.

'I've just been fixing Santa's lights – a very important job.' He winked.

'Is that in the crystal walkway?' Wilf asked.

'Yes, that's it. Lovely it is, all twinkly – you been in to see it?'

Wilf sighed. 'We can't afford it.'

'It's not right.' The man frowned. 'I remember back in the day the grotto was free. I used to bring my kids every year. Now it's only for the lucky few.'

'But Santa cares about all children,' Wilf said. 'I'm sure he does.'

And if I could just talk to Santa, Tizzy thought, *he could help Mum.*

'Here, tell you what, I'll unlock that service door and you

two can slip in and see Santa for free.'

'Really?' Wilf smiled.

Tizzy checked her watch. 'I guess we have time.'

The workman unlocked the hidden door and Tizzy and Wilf slipped away from the crowded toyshop into a dark corridor.

'Here you go,' the man said. He opened another small door. 'Duck through and keep walking – you'll be in the crystal walkway in a jiffy. Good luck and happy Christmas!' The door closed behind them and they heard the key turn in the lock.

Chapter Seven

No turning back. Tizzy gulped when she realised they were locked in. They had to go forward but the tunnel was dark. Taking a moment for their eyes to adjust, Tizzy and Wilf went on, picking their steps carefully until they saw light pricking around the outline of a doorway.

Pushing through, they joined the stream of rich visitors to Santa's Grotto.

Everyone had lollies and giant bags of candy.

Wilf nudged Tizzy. 'Can we get some?'

'We've no money.' Tizzy said, grabbing Wilf's hand and hurrying him along.

'Rudolph the Red-Nosed Reindeer' was playing over the loudspeaker as they entered the next chamber. It was built to look like a log cabin, with various workstations where robot elves with jolty movements were making toys. One elf was hammering a bolt into a toy train, while another was adding stuffing to a teddy bear's belly and a different elf tested the strings of a wooden puppet.

Studying the outer wall of the workshop, Wilf reached out to touch what looked like a log but felt smooth and shiny. 'It's plastic.' He made a face.

Tizzy shrugged. 'Like I said, things are often better in your imagination.'

'They're not making any boats.'

'Don't worry, it's just an example of the elves' work. You know they're making plenty of boats this year because Bob had samples direct from Santa's workshop.'

Leaving the robo-elves behind, Tizzy and Wilf passed through a doorway into a dark hall that opened onto the crystal walkway. The walls of the tunnel around them were lined with sparkling crystals and thousands of tiny twinkling lights.

'They look just like diamonds. It's so pretty. Mum would love this.' Tizzy tightened her hold on Wilf's hand, grateful that her little brother was by her side and that one day they could tell Mum and Dad about it.

'And look at that,' Wilf said. 'It's like the northern lights.' The crystal walkway opened out onto a larger domed area where green lights danced across a night sky. 'This is what it's like in the Arctic. The polar lights – aurora borealis.'

'Happy Christmas from Marmaduke's of Piccadilly!' a booming voice announced via a loudspeaker. 'You are now approaching the heart of Santa's Grotto. Please have your wristbands clearly visible to show to our trusty elves. Get ready to meet Father Christmas!' The bouncy tune of 'Jingle Bells' began to play at full volume.

Wristbands?

Tizzy and Wilf looked at each other, eyes wide with panic.

Wilf suggested they could try sneaking in.

'I don't think that'll work,' Tizzy said.

They searched around for an escape route.

'What if we go back the way we came?' Wilf said.

'We can't. The man locked the door, remember, and if we go back to the proper entrance, that elf with the lipstick knows we haven't got tickets.'

'Hey, are you going in or what?' A girl pointed an enormous lolly at Tizzy.

Not having a better plan, they followed the flow of lucky ticket holders towards the entrance to the main grotto. Ahead was a small opening with a Christmas tree on either side.

'Here Comes Santa Claus' was playing and this time there were two elves standing guard at the entrance, a tall young man and a woman who looked alert and tough like a terrier.

Everywhere Tizzy looked, people were pushing back their sleeves to show their wristbands.

We should never have done this.

She felt hot and panicky.

We shouldn't be here. What if they arrest us?

Desperately she searched in the dark, looking for another way out, as they inched forward in the line.

'Welcome to Santa's Grotto at Marmaduke's of Piccadilly.' The terrier-like lady elf smiled, showing small, ultra-white teeth. 'Please show your wristbands for admission to meet Father Christmas.'

'Quick!' Wilf pulled Tizzy to the left.

'Hey!' the lady elf shouted. 'They haven't got wristbands!'

The lanky male elf gave chase.

Tizzy looked over her shoulder. '*He's after us!* What now?'

'This way – I can see another exit.'

'Security to tunnel two!' The lanky elf was on a walkie-talkie, calling for back-up. 'We have two ticketless intruders without wristbands.'

Again, Wilf pulled Tizzy to the left. 'Quick, this way!'

'You're hurting my arm.'

'That giant elf is gaining on us.'

'Hey, you two, you're wasting your time – give yourselves up. Security is on the way.' The tall elf spoke again into his radio. 'Intruders approaching tunnel two. Security to the emergency exit. Returning to my post, over and out.'

'What's this?' Tizzy paused. They'd reached a service area. It was a drab grey corridor with a sign on a door that read 'Emergency Exit'.

'Shush, listen!' Wilf looked back over his shoulder.

They could hear heavy footsteps. 'Someone's coming!'

They pushed through the door and Tizzy scoured the room for options. On the other side she found a dark wooden hatch, carved like the wooden doors in the fancy toilets. This time the pattern was of rays streaming from a sun.

'It says Sunbeam Laundry.' Tizzy pulled at the hatch. 'I think it's a laundry chute, but it's shut tight.'

'"for staff use only".' Wilf read the sign underneath.

They heard a crackle, the sound of radio interference and muffled voices alongside footsteps – many heavy footsteps – and they were getting louder.

The door creaked open and a bald-headed mountain of a man in a neon jacket burst through the emergency exit.

'Stop right there!' he ordered. 'That's £25 each you owe and you'll have to spend £2000 in Marmaduke's. I hope you've been saving your pocket money.'

'Quick!' With all her strength, Tizzy pulled at the hatch and forced it open.

Wilf dived into the chute with Tizzy right behind him.

The security guard was almost onto her. Lunging, he grabbed her ankle.

Tizzy gave a mighty kick and scrambled free.

'Go!' she yelled.

Tizzy and Wilf held their breath and . . .

Chapter Eight

Whoosh!

Tizzy and Wilf launched themselves into the metal chute.

'Waaah!' they screamed.

Faster they went, zipping round a curve and ever onwards. Wilf with his backpack on hurtled head first in a dive, with Tizzy close behind.

'It's like one of those giant water slides!' she shouted, as they were whipped sideways to take another twist, then on and on, up and around, this way and that.

All at once, they were spun left and then right.

'I feel sick!' Wilf wailed.

Round and round, a little way up and a looong way down.

'I am never going on another ride anywhere!' It was worse than any rollercoaster Tizzy had ever been on, way faster and more furious, and extra fearsome because they were in the dark.

'I'm going to be sick,' Wilf said again.

'Don't you dare!'

'I can't help it.'

'It'll go all over me!'

'I'm doing my best to hold it in.'

'Make sure you do!'

They were jolted to one side, then the other.
'I'm so giddy,' Tizzy said.
'Me too. When will it end?'

They spun round again and again and hurtled onwards into the dark.

Tizzy shut her eyes and her stomach flipped. She was going too fast and she did not like it.

Warm air rushed up and hit them as they went faster still – until they were spat out . . .

. . . onto a soft mountain of squeaky stuff.

Pop! Pop! Pop!

'I think it's bubble wrap?' Tizzy felt around and squished a few more bubbles – *pop! pop! pop!* – and Wilf joined in.

'Stop!' Tizzy said. 'Someone might hear us.'

There was more light now, though it was only a faint glow.

'What is this place?'

They looked to be in some kind of big warehouse. There was a rumble and a clunking, metal on metal, and the sound of grinding machinery.

'It must be where deliveries arrive for Marmaduke's,' Wilf said.

'Let's take a closer look.' With a bit more popping, Tizzy slid to the floor. Set in the opposite wall stood a long line of doors, each one bearing a different sign.

'That one says Marmaduke's,' Wilf said.

'And the next one's Hamleys,' Tizzy said, 'and there's the Toy Station, the Entertainer, and the Enchanted Forest. They're all toyshops. This place we're in must be serving all these shops.' Tizzy walked along reading the labels. 'Look, that one's in New York, and there's the Lego Store in Berlin, and that shop says Dubai, and the next is Istanbul. These doors must be a way through to every toyshop in the world!'

Wilf paused. 'This says Mr Toys Toyworld in Sydney, Australia, that one is in Egypt and the next is in South Africa.'

'Do any of them say Cornwall?'

They thought of Bib and Bob's Toyshop back home. It was tiny compared to Marmaduke's, but Bob had a sample of nearly every toy direct from the elves.

Tizzy and Wilf followed the line of doors, searching for Bib and Bob's.

'We could see Mum and Dad,' Tizzy said. 'I miss them so much.'

Wilf nodded. 'I miss everything: Mum, Dad, my room, my bed and the cats – even the seagulls!'

Tizzy and Wilf jumped as a siren sounded and large brown boxes started to whizz off shelves and slide down metal chutes onto a conveyor belt to one of the doors, which opened to reveal a huge lift.

'Door 101,' came an announcement over a loudspeaker. 'Elevator to Mickey's Shop, Florida.'

'Did you hear that?' Wilf said. '*Florida – that's America!*'

They heard the whirr of a motor and a moment later a small buggy came around the corner and stopped at the door to Mickey's Shop. Two strong-looking men climbed out and checked on the boxes piling up.

'Who are they?' Wilf whispered.

'Shush! They might call security.'

The workers stopped what they were doing, turned around and stared.

Tizzy gulped. 'Hello, I wonder if you can help?' she said. 'We're a bit lost. Can you tell us the way back to Marmaduke's of Piccadilly? We need to go back to Dr Dushka's beauty clinic. That's where our grandma is. But we don't call her grandma – it's Gloriana.'

'Or we could go back to Bib and Bob's Toyshop in Cornwall – that would be even better,' Wilf said, 'because then we could see our mum and dad. They live nearby and we really miss them and the cats that come to visit. Our mum's quite poorly.'

The workers turned to one another and had what sounded like a heated debate.

'What are they saying?' Wilf asked.

'I've no idea. It doesn't sound English.'

Eventually, the men stopped and turned towards Tizzy and Wilf.

'Minik,' one of them said, tapping his chest.

'Seeglo,' the other one said.

'I'm Wilf and this is Tizzy.'

The men's shoulders started to shake and they put their hands over their mouths.

'They're laughing,' Wilf said. 'They think our names are funny.'

Minik walked off and Seeglo signalled that they should follow.

'Where's he going?' Wilf asked. 'Tell him we want to go through one of those doors and return to Marmaduke's or back home to Cornwall.'

'Excuse me,' Tizzy said, raising her hand, 'where are you going? We need to get back. It's nearly lunchtime and our grandma will be annoyed. She's really quite scary.'

Seeglo paused and said, 'Sinterklaas.'

'What?' Tizzy cupped her ear. 'Did you hear that?'

'That sounds like Santa Claus,' Wilf said.

'Sinterklaas.' Seeglo pointed to a door.

'He must mean Santa Claus,' Tizzy said.

'I *do* want to see Santa,' Wilf nodded.

'Maybe it's another way to the grotto in Marmaduke's?' Tizzy said. 'And then we can go back to Dr Dushka and find Gloriana.'

'Are we still in Marmaduke's?' Wilf asked.

'Sinterklaas,' Seeglo nodded.

'But we don't have wristbands.' Tizzy thought it best to be honest.

Seeglo raised his eyebrows. 'Sinterklaas?' he repeated.

'We'll just have to follow,' Tizzy said with a shrug. 'I mean, it's not as if we can go back up that laundry chute. It was way too slippery and it went on for ages. We must be somewhere deep in the basement of Marmaduke's.'

The noise of the sorting machine with its maze of chutes and conveyor belts filled the whole warehouse.

Clank! CRASH! Clank! SCREECH!

Tizzy and Wilf put their hands over their ears as they walked past.

On the other side, Seeglo stopped next to a doorway, took down some furry white trousers from a peg and pulled them on, followed by a thick white fur jacket. He tugged the hood over his head, and then pointed to an old wooden chest.

'It has the same carvings as up in Marmaduke's.' Wilf knelt down to feel the wood. 'Look, lots of ice, narwhals and a ship.' He pushed up the heavy lid and peered inside to find a whole heap more of thick furry mittens, hats and coats in all different sizes.

'But we already have coats on?' Tizzy zipped up her parka

and told Wilf to do the same.

'Take!' Minik insisted and they put on two lots each of mittens, coats and hats, and then he handed them each a torch with elastic straps.

'What do we do with these?' Tizzy asked.

Minik took one and fastened it over the hood on Tizzy's head.

Seeglo then lit a large storm lantern and opened the door to a burst of freezing cold air and blackness.

'Whoa!' Wilf gripped Tizzy's arm.

'Go now.' Minik stood back to let them through.

'It's so dark.' Tizzy's teeth chattered as she edged out into the night, fresh snow crunching underfoot.

'What's that?' Wilf tightened his grip on Tizzy's arm.

They heard the sound of howling. Was it the wind or . . . *something else*?

'Wolves?' Tizzy asked, with a crack in her voice.

'Come.' Seeglo didn't seem bothered. He held his lamp high and strolled over to a pack of huskies tethered to a sled.

Tizzy and Wilf looked on in awe.

'Wow!' Wilf counted the dogs. 'There are ten huskies.'

Seeglo signalled for Tizzy and Wilf to climb on to a seat at the back of the sled, where he laid blankets made of fur across their laps.

'Need keep warm,' he said. 'Long time to Sinterklaas.'

Tails up, the dogs barked with excitement.

After fastening the lamp to the sled, Seeglo stepped onto a ledge at the back and took the reins, shouting, 'Hup, hup!'

Minik gave them a wave goodbye and there was a sudden jolt as the huskies strained forward and the sled took off.

Pulling together, the dogs gathered speed.

Crossing the snow and ice, they ran, taking Tizzy and Wilf into the dark.

Chapter Nine

Gritting her teeth, Tizzy held on tight to the side of the sled as the dogs raced onwards.

'Faster!' Wilf shouted and on they sped across the frozen wastes.

'It's never this dark at home.' Tizzy searched for a hint of light.

'No sun.' Seeglo gestured towards the black sky.

'But it's only lunchtime.'

'No sun – winter.'

'You don't have streetlamps?' Tizzy asked.

Wind whipped their faces, making them retreat further into their hoods.

'Hup, hup!' Seeglo shouted to the dogs and Tizzy held on even tighter.

A few minutes later the dogs started barking.

'Can they see or smell something?' Tizzy asked.

'Fox.' Seeglo pointed to the right but Tizzy and Wilf couldn't make out the fox's white fur against the snow.

'I see it!' Wilf shouted as he spotted the eyes of the Arctic fox shining in the lamplight, and then it was gone.

On and on they went over miles of ice with only the sound of the howling wind, the dogs yelping and Seeglo's commands, until they swung to the side and came to a sudden halt. Tizzy and Wilf were nearly sent flying.

'Whoa, did we crash?' Wilf's hands hurt from grabbing on so tight.

The sled had stopped inches from a huge grey rock.

Tizzy leaned forward to take a better look. 'Can we go around it?'

There was a rumble and the rock trembled, though it was hard to tell in the dark.

'What is that?' Wilf asked.

'Rocks don't move?' Tizzy stood up, shining her headlamp on the massive lump.

Again the brownish-grey rock shook and swayed, and there was a flash of something light and white in the darkness.

'URRRGH!'

The great boulder made a deep bellowing sound and

turned to face them, and as it did so, two long curved tusks sliced the air like swords.

'A walrus.' Wilf's mouth dropped open.

Tizzy squeezed Wilf's hand. 'Do something, Seeglo.'

Seeglo lowered his eyes and bowed his head. 'Uglin,' he said.

'Uglin – is that the name of the walrus?' Wilf was confused.

There was a deep groan. The walrus raised himself up and bellowed.

Wilf gasped. 'What a noise it makes.'

The walrus's beady eyes looked down at Tizzy and Wilf and again he bellowed. '*URRRGH, URRRGH!*'

Tizzy and Wilf trembled as Seeglo laughed. 'He say, you small.'

Tizzy made a face. 'I think you'll find we're average for our ages. I mean there are taller people in my class but there are lots who are smaller.'

'*URRRGH, URRRGH?*' Once more the walrus hollered, making Tizzy's innards quake.

'He ask if you children,' Seeglo explained.

Tizzy shrugged. 'Yes, of course we're children.'

The walrus's head whipped to one side with displeasure and his growl grew even deeper. '*URRRGH!*'

'He say not right.'

'What do you mean?' Tizzy frowned. 'I don't understand.'

'*URRRGH, URRRGH, URRRGH!*' the walrus howled.

'No place for children,' Seeglo translated. 'You not welcome.'

'That's rude. It's not as if we asked to come here.' Tizzy folded her arms.

The walrus continued to roar.

'Uglin say you want Sintaklaas.'

'We're here by accident,' Tizzy said. 'We didn't mean to come. We were on our way back to our grandma – I mean Gloriana (she hates being called grandma). It's nearly lunchtime and she's going to be so angry when she finds out we're not there. Where is Marmaduke's exactly? Is it far from here?'

Bigger and louder bellows shook the frozen world.

'He say no accident,' Seeglo said.

'We don't even know where we are,' Tizzy said.

The walrus tilted his hairy blubbery chin and his roars rang out again.

'He ask, what you see?'

'It's so dark.' Tizzy shook her head. 'It's hard to see anything.'

'There's nothing but snow and ice,' Wilf said, 'which makes me think we must be in the extreme north. Is this the Arctic?'

More tremble-inducing groans from the walrus, along with a hard pebble-eyed stare.

Seeglo continued to speak for the walrus. 'You ask for grotto?'

'We did, as in Marmaduke's of Piccadilly – you know, the famous department store in London,' Tizzy explained. 'That's where we need to be right now.'

Terrible, ground-shaking thundering bellows sounded from the mighty creature.

'Uglin say one *true* grotto.'

'Where is that?' Tizzy asked.

'Is this the North Pole?' Wilf stared into the surrounding darkness.

The walrus heaved his gigantic bulk around, and turning his back on them, blasted out more terrifying cries into the night.

'You on Elf Road,' Seeglo stated.

'This is Elf Road!' Tizzy squealed. 'It's nothing like how I imagined it. I mean, I can't see cars or streetlamps and where are the houses and house numbers? We need to find number 123.'

The walrus snorted as if Tizzy had said something stupid. '*URRRGH, URRRGH!*'

'He say, no houses,' Seeglo said helpfully.

The walrus grumbled some more and lolloped away, his vast bulk sending up a flurry of snowy spray as he shifted with quite surprising speed.

'I'm so confused,' Tizzy said. 'Can you take us back to Marmaduke's?'

Seeglo shrugged. 'Sinterklaas, yes.'

'Yes!' Wilf whooped. 'You mean at the grotto in Marmaduke's?'

'Hup, hup!' Seeglo shouted.

And the huskies took off once again across the frozen ice.

Tizzy and Wilf clung to each other and onwards they went.

'It's like we've started something that can't be stopped,' Tizzy fretted, 'and we're not even welcome here.'

I wish we could go home and see Mum. I hope she's all right.

A tear froze upon Tizzy's cheek. She wiped it away and clamped the front of her hood shut, trying to block out the cold, the dark and the fear.

Chapter Ten

Shivering, Tizzy hid her face in her hood, while Seeglo urged the dogs on, towards what or where it was unclear.

The chill wind made Wilf's eyes water and he blinked back tears, keen to see into the inky blackness.

Onwards they dashed, faster and further, until the dark ahead was pierced with tiny dots of light.

'Wow!' Wilf nudged his sister. 'Tizzy, you have to see.'

'What is it?'

'All the lights, look! They're amazing.'

Tizzy peeped from within her hood. 'It's like thousands of tiny stars have floated down.'

'What is it?' Wilf asked. 'Where are they coming from?'

'Hup, hup!' Seeglo hurried the dogs on, and as they drew nearer, they could see coloured lights strung like twinkly washing lines between heavy funnels and radio masts.

Wilf gasped. 'It's an icebreaker, a real expedition cruise ship – the world's toughest. Look at the size of it!'

'What would a ship be doing out here in the middle of nowhere?' The cold air stung Tizzy's eyes as she stared. Wilf was right. A large squat ship sat like a giant beached whale in the ice, its top bathed in gentle colour against the surrounding dark.

'It's been decorated for Christmas,' Tizzy said. 'Is it a Christmas ship?'

The huskies ran towards the lights and Seeglo steered them so close they could read the ship's name painted across its hull.

'It's called the *Arctic Star*. Is this where Santa lives?' Tizzy asked.

Seeglo nodded and pointed. 'Sinterklaas.'

Wilf shook his head. 'I never knew he had a ship.'

'No build here,' Seeglo said.

'You mean you can't build out on the ice?' Wilf said.

Seeglo nodded. 'No build.' Slowing the dogs, he pulled up alongside a covered metal gangway leading up from the vast ocean of ice and onto the ship.

The huskies ground to a halt and Seeglo grunted as he nodded in the direction of a metal gate at the entrance to the gangway.

The ship looked bright and inviting as it sat there trapped

in the ice and the darkness beyond, but what if no one let them on board?

'You'll wait for us here?' Tizzy's heart was racing.

Seeglo pointed again towards the gangway. 'Go!'

'What if we can't get on the ship?'

He nodded towards the ship and gave another grunt.

'I don't know. There might be no one there.'

Seeglo waved towards a small box at the entrance to the gangway.

Wilf stepped off the sled to take a closer look. 'I think it's an entryphone. The button looks like it's iced up.'

Tizzy nudged him out of the way and jabbed the button with her finger. 'Hello?'

The entryphone crackled and after a few seconds, a squeaky voice said, 'Not today, thank you.'

Tizzy tried again. 'Hello there! I wonder if you can help us?'

'Whatever it is you're selling, we don't want it – never have and never will, so there. Goodbye!'

'We're not selling anything,' Tizzy said.

'It's lunchtime – how rude to turn up at lunchtime. Go away!'

'We can't,' Tizzy said. 'Please, you must help us.'

'I'd rather eat my lunch, thanks. What do you want?'

'We've come all the way from London.'

'Well, go back to London then. There you are, that was helpful.'

'Um, is Santa there?'

'This is boring. My soup's getting cold. What are you going to do about that?'

'I'm sorry about your soup, it's just I need to know if this is where we can find Father Christmas?'

'What a silly question! This is the North Pole. Who else would live out here? Think about it, it's the only place the poor guy gets any peace – and now you've turned up to disturb him.'

'We did ask to visit Santa's Grotto, but we had no idea we'd end up here!'

'Take my advice, kiddo – go back to where you came from and you know how it goes: be good, fall asleep early on Christmas Eve and Santa will come visit you, and on Christmas morning it'll be smiles all round. Perfect!'

Wilf now joined in. 'The thing is, we're here now and Seeglo keeps telling us to go. It feels like we're not welcome anywhere.'

'You weren't invited so of course you're not welcome. I mean, do you normally just turn up out of the blue?'

'We didn't plan to come here,' said Tizzy. 'We were being chased and got lost – and the next thing we knew we were on a dog sled in the Arctic!'

Distracted by barking, she glanced round and saw Seeglo turn the sled, ready to leave.

'What are you doing?' Tizzy's heart thumped faster than ever. 'You can't leave us!'

'Hup, hup!'

'Hey!' Tizzy shouted. 'Stop!'

Seeglo smiled and waved. 'Hup, hup!' he ordered. And the huskies pulled together, gathering speed to blast off across the frozen ice.

'Stop! Seeglo, WAIT!'

'Hup, hup!' They went even faster.

'Seeglo! No! Don't go!'

Oblivious to Tizzy's cries, Seeglo's shouts of 'hup, hup' soon faded to a whisper as he disappeared into darkness.

'How could he leave us like that?' Tears welled in Tizzy's eyes. 'What now?' She looked around, desperate for an answer as the tears froze on her cheeks.

Wilf was shaking uncontrollably. 'It's too cold – even my

eyebrows have frosted up. We'll die out here.'

Tizzy pressed the buzzer on the entryphone and this time kept her finger on it.

The intercom crackled and the squeaky voice said, 'Enough already! Haven't you gone yet?'

'You have to help. He's left us here in the middle of nowhere.'

'Who has?'

'Seeglo.'

'See what?'

'Seeglo – he's gone. We're stuck here all alone and it's freezing. *We're going to die!*'

'That old trick – making out your life's at risk and only I can help.' There was a loud sigh. 'Very well, climb on board if you must, but don't think you're staying. I've got soup to eat and I'll slurp away before it gets cold.'

A buzzer sounded and the metal gate inched open.

'Quick!' Tizzy lunged for the gate. 'Go through before he changes his mind.'

Pushing through onto the ship's gangway, Wilf found himself on the long gentle ramp up to the deck.

Behind him, Tizzy grabbed for the handrail as the gangway shook beneath her feet. 'It's wobbly! Do you think it's safe?' The rail was icy to the touch, even through her gloves, and the light from her head torch shone on rows of glittering icicles hanging from the sides.

'It's like the crystal walkway at Marmaduke's,' she said.

'No, this is better than the crystal walkway,' Wilf insisted. 'This is the real thing.'

The surface of the gangplank sparkled with frost, reflecting the glow from their head torches and the coloured fairy lights overhead.

'It's so pretty.' Tizzy almost forgot about the cold and how scared she was until she slipped and started to wail.

'Are you okay?' Wilf helped her up and they shuffled on towards the deck.

From the top, the ship seemed to float like a brilliant island in an endless sea of frozen darkness.

Tizzy closed her eyes for a moment to catch her breath. *Please let this be okay*, she thought.

'I've found the way in.' Wilf waved towards a metal door. 'But there's no bell or door knocker.'

'That's strange.' Tizzy tapped on the metal. 'Hello? Can you let us in?'

'They'll never hear that.' Wilf banged on the door with his fist and yelled, 'HELLO!'

The door opened a fraction.

'Quick,' said the same squeaky voice as before, 'and shut the door behind you.'

A small green mitten peeked out from the crack in the doorway and beckoned them in.

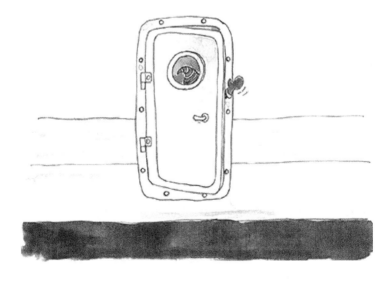

Chapter Eleven

Inside, the ship walls were lined with wooden panelling, strung with more fairy lights.

Wilf pulled off his glove and touched one of the panels. 'It's real, not like that fake log cabin at Marmaduke's.'

There was a distant jingling of bells and Tizzy and Wilf sniffed hungrily at the fragrant aroma of frying fish.

'Smells like Dad's cooking,' Tizzy said with a sigh.

'I hope Dad's remembering to feed the cats,' Wilf said.

'He'll throw them the scraps, I know he will.' Tizzy took off the furs from the warehouse and her parka. 'It's so hot in here! Where is everyone?'

Wilf took off his outdoor gear, and spotted a piece of paper on a table. 'The note says, "Gone to lunch. If hungry, follow the red route to the dining room".'

Tizzy had expected the owner of the little green mitten to be there to greet them. Instead there were corridors leading off in every direction. 'This side has red tape.' Tizzy pointed to a coloured line fixed at waist level along the corridor on the right.

'I don't know about you, but I am hungry.' Wilf marched ahead. 'Come on!'

'This means it's already lunchtime. Gloriana will be going crazy,' Tizzy fretted.

'Not much we can do about that.' Wilf was on a mission and was heading directly to the dining room.

Following the red tape, they hurried down the narrow wood-panelled corridor and turned right, then left, then left again and down a flight of steps.

The line of red guided them ever closer towards the delicious fishy smells until they ended up outside a huge set of carved wooden doors.

'I love that,' Wilf said, staring at the pattern of snow-covered pine trees. 'They're the same style as those doors we saw in Marmaduke's –I reckon it's a Christmas forest.'

Beyond the doors they could hear chatter and the *clink-clack* of clashing cutlery. Tizzy took a deep breath and eased the door open.

Inside was a large dining hall with rows of long tables and benches filled with hundreds of elves, all dressed in green. Gradually, table by table, the elves paused, spoons and forks halfway to their mouths. The room fell silent as everyone looked over.

'Who are they?' said the nearest elf.

One with curly hair got to his feet. '*What* are they, more like?'

'They're too big for elves,' said an elf with long eyelashes.

'Are they intruders?' One elf hid behind his hands.

Another elf almost choked on his drink.

'For goodness' sake, Cedric, pull yourself together,' the next elf said.

Cedric's eyes watered as he jabbed his finger towards Tizzy and Wilf and tried to get enough breath to say something.

'What is it? Spit it out,' the elf next to him said.

'Look, look!' Cedric rasped.

Wilf hid behind Tizzy. 'What's the matter with him?'

'He's laughing at us.' Tizzy felt her face go red as she checked what she was wearing. *Why is he laughing like that?* She felt around in case she had a bogey or was dribbling.

I wish we'd never come here, she thought, *even though we'd like to meet Father Christmas.*

Cedric was crying with laughter, with other elves now joining in.

'See that?' Cedric pointed. 'Look at their EARS!'

'Hahaha,' another elf laughed. 'Their ears are all round at the top!'

Dozens of elves stood up to get a better look and others edged forward.

'Why are their ears like that? What's WRONG with them?'

The elves laughed themselves silly, clutching their sides and rolling on the floor it was so funny.

One young elf stood on his chair and held up his hand for silence. 'Hang on a minute!' he shouted. 'MAYBE THEY'RE NOT ELVES!'

'I wish they'd stop laughing.' Wilf's voice was wobbly.

Tizzy clenched her fists. 'Excuse me,' she said loudly, 'I think you're all being very rude!'

There was a brief hush and then the elves collapsed in giggles again, until one elf with knee-high red and white striped socks came forward. 'Shush! That's enough, everybody – quieten down.' He gestured for everyone to behave themselves and then turned to address Tizzy and Wilf. 'On behalf of the elf community, I would like to apologise.'

He turned back to the elves. 'We have visitors. This is what visitors look like. Hey, and more to the point, don't forget Santa's ears are rounded.'

There was a flurry of whispers and someone had hiccups.

The elf with the red and white socks turned back to Tizzy and Wilf and said, 'You're our first visitors ever and you're a bit of a surprise to us all.'

'You've never had visitors before?' Tizzy was confused.

Stripy Socks shrugged. 'We've heard visitors take up a lot of time and we're very busy.' He had green mittens hanging from his belt. *Was he the one who had let them on to the ship?*

He turned to address the other elves again. 'These visitors are from London, and it's only a guess but I think they may be *children*.'

There were more gasps and another round of whispers.

'Children!' Cedric exclaimed. 'Is that what you are?'

Tizzy and Wilf nodded. 'Yes, of course we're children.'

'They don't look that different,' said an elf with red hair.

'What are they doing here?' an elf at the back said, folding his arms.

'Fair question,' Stripy Socks said. 'What are you doing here?'

Tizzy shrugged. 'We're trying to get back to Marmaduke's. We have to meet Gloriana and she'll be doing her nut.'

'None of that makes any sense,' Stripy Socks said. 'Are you talking in code?'

'They're looking for Santa,' an older elf said. 'It's obvious.'

Stripy Socks shook his head. 'Santa is far too busy for guests.'

'We only wanted to go to the grotto in the shop,' Wilf explained. 'Do you know Marmaduke's of Piccadilly in London? That's where we were and then all of a sudden we ended up here.'

'That's what happens when you look for the one and only, numero uno, Real Genuine Grotto.' Stripy Socks frowned. 'Imagine what would happen if every kid turned up looking for Santa – we'd get nothing done, no toys would be made and Christmas would have to be cancelled!'

'We're in the way, I can see that,' Tizzy said, 'and we'd really like to go, but Seeglo left so we're stranded here and we don't know what to do.'

The elf's face softened. 'Well, you're here now and it's just the two of you. It is just you two, isn't it?' Tizzy and Wilf nodded. 'We'd better get you fed.' He took them over to the café counter and passed them each a bowl of soup and then some elves made space for the children to sit down.

'You kids got names?' Stripy Socks asked.

'I'm Tizzy and this is Wilf.'

'Ootah.'

'Sorry, did you say Ootah?' Tizzy thought the name sounded familiar but she couldn't remember where she'd heard it before.

'My name's Ootah, as in "ooh, ta very much".'

Wilf put his hand over his mouth to stifle a giggle.

'My ma put a lot of love and care into choosing my name. It ain't funny.'

Tizzy scowled at Wilf. 'Sorry, he didn't mean to laugh,' she said. 'We know how you feel – people sometimes laugh at our names too.'

'Phew, it's hot in here,' Wilf said. 'It's hard to believe we're in the Arctic.'

'Does this ship go anywhere else?' Tizzy asked.

'It must do,' Wilf said, 'or there'd be no point in it being a superior, specially designed expedition cruise ship.'

Ootah nodded. 'The *Arctic Star* is one of a kind and it certainly does move. Sadly, it's getting easier as the ice is melting. People need to take more care of the Earth.'

'Can you take us home?' Tizzy asked. 'Please?'

Bing bong! sounded a loudspeaker. 'Squadron Two to the Doll Room. Late rush on dolls – calling all Squadron Two. I repeat, Squadron Two to the Doll Room.'

'But I've only had a short lunch break,' Cedric moaned.

'Can't let the kids down – back to work, Cedric,' Ootah ordered.

An elf sporting a tartan bow tie came to the table and passed a document to Ootah, who in turn passed it on to Tizzy.

'If you wanna see Santa, you gotta sign this on page seventy-three.'

Tizzy read aloud, '"The Official Santa's Secrets Act". The print is so small I can barely read it.'

'Don't read it. We ain't got time for that.'

'But you should always read anything before you sign.'

'That's right, sound advice, and you should never travel to the Arctic alone, or talk to elves you don't know, but you did that and that already. You are way out of your depth, kiddo. You wanna go further and meet the great man himself, or are you gonna be sensible, sign nothing, and get thrown out onto the ice?'

'Well, when you put it like that.' Tizzy took the tiny elf-sized pen and signed in her best loopy handwriting before passing it to Wilf. 'Out of interest, what does it say?'

'It says if you speak a word to ANYONE about what you see here today, you'll never get another Christmas present for the rest of your days.'

Tizzy and Wilf gulped.

'Christmas makes winter wonderful,' Wilf said.

'Winter without Christmas would be like summer without ice cream,' Tizzy said, 'or without swimming at the beach.'

'I'm not sure I get what you're saying but I'm gonna nod anyhow.' Ootah put a phone to his pointy ear. 'The big guy's not ready for you yet, so in the meantime I'll show you round. This way.' Ootah went ahead and Tizzy and Wilf hurried to catch up as he led them along a corridor painted with a mural of pine trees. 'Notice there were no trees out there?'

'It was too dark to see anything,' Wilf said.

'No light until February or March.'

'Are you serious?' Tizzy said.

'No light in winter, not here.'

'I'd hate that,' Tizzy said.

'Me too,' Wilf said.

'Santa misses the trees. He likes trees, especially Christmas trees. All right, this is Dolls HQ.'

The room was lined with shelves stacked with boxes containing every kind of doll the children had ever seen, along with many more.

'I don't really like dolls,' Tizzy said.

'Well, millions of kids do like 'em,' Ootah said, 'and this is where we make 'em.' There was an assembly line with elves stationed at intervals to add arms, legs, eyes and hair.

'That doll wees.' Tizzy pointed to a baby doll with more hair than any tiny tot she'd ever seen.

An elf was testing the crying mechanism on another doll.

Wilf put his hands over his ears.

'Too noisy, huh?' Ootah led them through Doll HQ to the next room, where there was another assembly line creating robot dinosaurs.

'This is more like it,' Wilf said, but Ootah was already moving on to the next chamber which was full of toy vehicles: cars, trains, planes and boats.

Wilf's mouth fell open at the sight of elves operating remote-controlled boats on a pool in the corner, set into the top of a large table.

Tizzy smiled. 'You have no idea how much he likes boats.'

Wilf went in for a closer look. 'That's a Sea Ray, and that one's good for deep-sea fishing and there's a rescue boat. I really hope I get one of those.'

'Fingers crossed,' Tizzy said.

'OK, moving on – we have a lot of departments to see.'

Ootah strode ahead.

'How many departments are there?' Tizzy asked.

Ootah rolled his eyes as he counted. 'One hundred and twenty-three at the last count.'

Tizzy understood at last. 'That's why your address is 123 Elf Road.'

'Monkeys!' Wilf pointed towards the sound of chimpanzees.

'That's the Jungle Room.' Ootah held back knitted vines to allow them through.

'Tigers and lions – I love lions!' Wilf smiled at the mounds of stuffed animals: big cats, snakes, orangutans, elephants, aardvarks and hyenas. Wilf stroked a plush giraffe.

'That on your Christmas list?' Ootah asked.

Wilf nodded. 'I'm hoping for a mother and baby.'

'He likes things to be in pairs or even numbers,' Tizzy explained.

'Well, one, two, whatever, you ain't gonna be able to take it now.'

Wilf looked teary as he hugged the giraffe and Tizzy guessed he was thinking of Mum back home in Cornwall and Dad caring for her. Maybe he was even thinking of Gloriana in her tall grey house with no Christmas decorations.

Christmas might not happen, Tizzy thought. *What if Mum's illness is getting worse?*

She put her arm round Wilf as she unpeeled his fingers from around the giraffe's soft body and placed the toy back on the pile.

'Here you go.' She passed Wilf a tissue.

Ootah winked. 'Don't worry, kiddo, if it's on your list . . .'

'Do you have computer games?' Tizzy asked.

'Down a floor. Follow me.'

Deep in the ship's belly there was a background hum of machines, interrupted by the odd *clank* and *clang*.

'It's the heating system,' Ootah explained.

Keying in a special code, he tapped the side of his nose. 'Top secret down here,' he said. 'They work three years ahead.'

Inside, serious-looking elves were staring intently at computer screens.

'Eggy is head of design down here,' Ootah said, introducing the games expert.

Eggy jumped in his seat. 'Don't creep up on me like that!'

'Sorry, Eggy, can you tell us what you're working on?'

Eggy looked sideways at Tizzy and Wilf. 'Who are they?'

'This is Tizzy and Wilf – they're kids. Our first visitors.' Ootah smiled. 'Eggy doesn't get out much. He's here all day, every day.'

'Why are they different sizes?'

'I don't know.' Ootah frowned. 'Why are you different sizes?'

'I'm older than Wilf,' Tizzy said. 'Are elves all the same size?'

'Pretty much.' Eggy shrugged and returned to his computer screen.

'Eggy creates virtual reality,' Ootah said.

Eggy hit a few strokes on his keyboard and his screen filled with a fantasy battle between a roaring giant Cyclops and a virtual Eggy.

Tizzy thought of the BuzzKidz Game Player she was hoping to receive. It no longer seemed so amazing compared with Eggy's new game.

'We'll leave him to it,' Ootah said. 'We've another 118 departments to visit.'

Tizzy smiled and asked, 'So what's next?'

'The LCR.' Ootah picked up his pace.

'What's that?'

'The Letter Control Room. It's where we check what everyone's asked for.'

Tizzy gulped as she remembered she'd sent two letters.

'Hey, we can call up your letter.' Ootah grinned. 'I'd love to see what you asked for and make sure you get what you want.'

Tizzy's cheeks burned. What would Ootah think of the fact she'd submitted not one, but two letters to Santa?

'Do we have to go there? I mean Santa may well be ready for us by now?'

'He's not ready yet, trust me, I know what the Big Guy is like – he needs his rest after lunch. Okay, let's go check your letter.'

Ootah led them down several corridors, turning left, then right, then left again until they reached a door labelled 'LCR'.

Tizzy gulped. *Fingers crossed they haven't connected my two letters.*

She knew she'd gone red because she was hot and her

heart was thumping, but what could she do? She was stuck, trapped on an icebreaker ship at the North Pole, thousands of miles from home – and all because they'd disobeyed Gloriana and sneaked off to visit Santa's Grotto.

Chapter Twelve

The Letter Control Room was a large office filled with elves sat at desks with computers, surrounded by sacks full of mail.

One elf took letters from the first sack, sorted them into piles and then shared them out between the desks, where the seated elves opened each one, read it and started typing.

'Do they have to input all the information?' Tizzy asked.

'Of course. Santa needs names, addresses, ages and requests.'

'What if—' Tizzy paused. There was a lump in her throat and her heart was beating fast. 'What if someone sends more than one letter?'

'Well, that would be odd.' Ootah frowned, but relayed Tizzy's question to the foreman.

The foreman, a stout elf with a deeply lined forehead and a downturned mouth, grunted, 'More than one letter?'

Tizzy knew she'd turned red. Wilf had been right – she should never have written a second time.

'More than one letter? Are you serious? No one should write more than once. You, girl – the one with the messy hair!' The foreman was staring at Tizzy.

Hot tears welled in her eyes. *Why, oh why, did I write twice?*

'Why did you ask that? What's your name?' he said. 'Did you write two letters?'

Tizzy gulped.

'Sorry, I didn't quite catch that. What's your name?'

'It's Tizzy Biff.'

'Where are you from, Tizzy Biff?'

'London.' She thought that if she made out she lived at Grandma Gloriana's instead of her home in Cornwall she might get away with it.

'Where in London?'

'Elbert Crescent.'

'Listen up, everybody,' the foreman shouted, 'key in Tizzy Biff, Elbert Crescent, London, and tell me what you get.'

Twenty or so elves tapped away at their keyboards, while Tizzy blew up at her damp straggly hair, resigned to being found out.

'Got it, boss!' an elf shouted. 'This is her.'

A siren sounded and a red light flashed.

The piercing noise made the elves cover their pointy ears while the foreman shook his head. 'I thought as much. You're one of *them*, aren't you?'

'Sorry,' Tizzy said, 'one of what?'

'One of the greedies – *Spoiltus Braticus*,' the foreman said.

Ootah shook his head and looked down at his curly-toed shoes.

Am I greedy? Tizzy bit her lip as she thought of the cramped room she shared with Wilf back in Cornwall. They had toys crafted from driftwood alongside one or two precious gifts purchased from Bib and Bob's Toyshop.

'How many letters we got?' the foreman asked.

'It's coming up with two,' the keyboard operator said. 'Not as bad as the one I had earlier. Some girl called Beatrice Bling sent in FIVE. Can you believe that? *Five letters!* That's five letters listing more and more gifts: cuddly bears, hair curlers, make-up, a karaoke machine, a waffle maker, roller skates, a tutu, an electric guitar, a horse and a *swimming pool* – the requests went on and on . . .'

Tizzy let her hair fall forward to hide her face. Gazing down at her shoes, she wished she could run home to sit by the fire with Mum and Dad.

'One long letter listing requests not enough for you, kid?' The foreman was still staring and it reminded her of the mean ticket inspector on the train to London. 'You one of those kids who wants everything she sees?'

'It's not like that.'

'I bet she eats two desserts,' another elf said, 'and *heaps* of cakes and candy.'

'Do you know how hard Santa works?' The foreman shook his head. 'That guy, he's the best, but boy, does he get worn out. I mean things were bad enough anyhow, but kids now want everything they see and send in letter after letter asking for more toys and gadgets, and we have to deal with it. It's a struggle dealing with one letter per kid, let alone two or three or *more*.'

A skinny elf nodded. 'Yeah, *and* we have to match them up.'

'It's getting harder every year,' said another. 'Sometimes we don't even get a lunch break.'

'We should go on *strike*!' a blonde elf said.

A young elf folded his arms. 'Yeah, let's stop typing up these letters!'

An elf with her hair in bunches nodded. 'We should stop making toys.'

Another lady elf agreed. 'The kids are too greedy – we should stop everything.'

'Yeah, why don't we stop?' said another.

The elves stood up. They were all talking at once, complaining and shaking their fists. 'DOWN WITH GREEDY KIDS!' they shouted.

'Down with ALL KIDS!' yelled the one with bunches.

'Children are *cruel* to elves,' said an old elf.

'Elves have rights too!' shouted an elf with gold teeth.

A curly-haired elf said, 'I want an afternoon nap!'

'STOP CRUELTY TO ELVES!'

'I want a tea break and cookies!' said another.

'Ban the second letters!'

A young pointy-nosed elf ran to the front. 'I know, I know, let's CANCEL CHRISTMAS!'

The elves all paused to consider this idea.

The curly-haired elf shouted, 'Yeah, CANCEL CHRISTMAS!'

'Cancel Christmas – it's simple,' said the old elf. 'Why didn't I think of that?'

'CANCEL CHRISTMAS!' They all joined in, dancing round the room, waving their fists as they sang. 'Cancel Christmas! Cancel Christmas! Cancel Christmas!'

'Down with the greedies!'

'STOP CRUELTY TO ELVES!'

'Down with kids!'

'We're on strike!'

'CHRISTMAS IS CANCELLED!'

Chapter Thirteen

Pandemonium spread through the ship.

Elves ran from room to room chanting, 'Equal rights for elves! Down with kids! CANCEL CHRISTMAS!'

Ootah shook his head. 'Look what you've started.'

'It's all a misunderstanding,' Tizzy cried. 'If you'd just let me explain?'

Elves ran through the corridors, shoving past Tizzy, Wilf and Ootah.

'Hey, steady on! We need to do something.' Ootah followed a group of elves into the Doll Room.

Cedric was standing on one of the tables addressing his fellow team members. 'It's time to put our feet up. We want proper lunch breaks!'

'Down with greedy kids!' an elf shouted.

'Let's go on strike!'

Cedric agreed. 'CHRISTMAS IS CANCELLED!'

'Are you crazy?' the team leader said, tapping his foot. 'We've got a late rush on dolls. We need to make at least a hundred an hour. I need everyone back to work *pronto*.'

'Stuff it!' Cedric pumped his fist. 'We're fighting back. EQUAL RIGHTS FOR ELVES!'

The Doll Room team leader groaned. 'This is all kinds of bad. Santa won't like it one bit.'

But the elves didn't care. Cheering, they joined in with chants of 'CANCEL CHRISTMAS!'

'Down with greedies!' Cedric shouted. 'No more letters, no more toys.'

'Equal rights for elves!' yelled one of his friends.

'CANCEL CHRISTMAS!'

'Long lunch breaks for all!'

'Stop cruelty to ELVES!'

The elves were shaking their fists and stamping their feet.

'No more letters, no more lists!' they chanted as they took off into the corridor, spreading out to all 123 departments.

'Down with greedies!'

'We need proper lunch breaks!'

'Stop cruelty to elves!'

'Please, there's been a misunderstanding,' Tizzy tried to explain again. 'It's not how it seems.'

Ootah shook his head. 'I wish I'd never let you on board the *Arctic Star*. Ever since you arrived, the ship's gone crazy.'

'Can we go back to the Letter Control Room?' Tizzy pleaded. 'I think it could help.'

Wilf reached for Tizzy's hand.

'This is a crisis.' Ootah looked worried. 'I don't know what to do. We're so behind schedule. Christmas is well and truly cancelled whether we like it or not.'

Leaving the Doll Room, Ootah visited the Jungle Room, the Dinosaur Department, and Model Trains, and everywhere he went, it was the same. Elves were waving banners and shouting, 'Equal rights for ELVES! No more letters, no more

TOYS! DOWN WITH KIDS!'

Again Ootah shook his head. 'I had no idea the elves were so unhappy.'

'Tired of long hours, tired of greedy kids!' an elderly elf moaned.

'Short lunches make unhappy elves!' A tiny elf shook her fist.

'CANCEL CHRISTMAS!'

The whole ship was full of furious, stomping, fist-waving elves.

'Calm down, everyone!' Ootah pleaded. 'Let's talk about this. We can sort it out.'

'Sort yourself out, traitor. This way, everyone!' Cedric and the elves stormed off to the Letter Control Room and Ootah, Tizzy and Wilf were left with no choice but to follow on behind.

'Greedy kids don't deserve presents.'

'Let's destroy the letters!' Cedric shouted.

'Ignore all demands,' said another. 'Rip 'em up!'

Cheering, the elves grabbed the sacks full of letters and emptied them all over the floor.

'Hahaha, dump the letters!' Cheering, the elves stomped all over the unopened mail, jumping up and down and dirtying the envelopes with their curly-toed shoes.

'WHAT ON EARTH?!!'

A very loud, deep roar stopped the elves in their tracks.

'What is all this commotion?' The voice was drawing nearer, along with heavy footsteps. 'I have NEVER heard such a rabble! It woke me from my nap and you *know* how much I like my nap.'

The elves held their breath.

At last there was hush.

All eyes were on the door, while a few elves scrabbled on the floor, picking up letters and shoving them into sacks.

Wilf covered his ears, and Tizzy wished she were home in their small cosy cottage with Mum and Dad and the visiting cats.

'What is this hullabaloo?' Again it was that loud bellowing voice.

The foreman waved his arms. 'Quiet, everyone – *shush*!'

Most of the elves paid attention, though a few continued to grumble.

'What is all this fuss? I have NEVER heard such noise.' The raging grew louder still as the heavy footsteps drew closer.

'What the heck can the matter be?'

'*Shush*, quieten down.' Waving his arms, the foreman tried to silence his crew.

There was a moment's hush before the door burst open.

First a large red belly came into view, and then a whole figure filled the doorway in a way that no teeny-tiny elf could ever achieve.

'*It's him!*' Tizzy whispered.

'It's really, really him.' Wilf's eyes were wide and his mouth fell open.

It was Santa Claus indeed, in all his white-bearded glory, but he looked gruff, gloomy, grumpy and totally, absolutely, completely cheesed off.

'Well?' he said. 'What have you noisy elves got to say for yourselves?' His bright blue eyes scanned the room.

Stepping back, Tizzy and Wilf crouched down in the corner.

The foreman stepped forward. 'I'm so sorry, sir – a little misunderstanding got a bit out of hand.'

'Go on,' Santa said, stroking his beard, 'do tell me more.'

Feeling hot from her scalp to her toes, Tizzy broke out in a sweat at the thought of what was about to be said.

'There was a double list, sir – someone sent a second letter – as in *two from the same kid*. You know how it is these days. They don't know when to stop. They ask for everything and more, and then they spot extra stuff they want – the latest video game, new trainers, a dinosaur – and they write again.'

'It's worse than ever.' Santa shook his head. 'What are we to do?'

An elf raised his hand. 'I say we miss out the kids that write more than once.'

'That seems harsh.' Santa went back to stroking his long white beard as if it were a favourite pet. 'I wouldn't want to be mean – I'm not a mean fellow – but we have to draw the line somewhere. Who's the latest culprit?'

Tizzy crept as far back as she could against the wall. If only she could fall right through to another room where no one would ask about letters or Christmas lists.

The grumpiest elf pointed. 'That's her – she's the one. She wrote twice.'

Santa turned his big bearded head in her direction. 'Goodness me, child, what were you thinking?' His bushy eyebrows lowered with disappointment. 'It's hard enough to deliver all the things on each child's list, plus the surprises, let alone when a kid writes twice or more. I'm a busy man with a sleigh so heavy it's at breaking point. Why on *earth* would you write twice?'

'She's gone red, look – even her little rounded ears are red,' said a mean-looking elf, pointing at Tizzy. 'A greedy girl like that should be embarrassed at herself.'

'Don't worry.' Wilf squeezed Tizzy's hand. 'I know you're not greedy.'

'What was that?' Santa asked. 'You, the little guy, what did you say?'

Wilf inched forward. 'I said, she's not greedy or spoilt.'

'What makes you think that?'

'I know because she's my sister, Tizzy.'

'Well, young man, it's noble of you to defend your big sister, but the simple truth is she has sent two letters and therefore double the requests. In my long experience, when someone writes twice, it means only one thing.'

'Greedy, so greedy,' the elves muttered. 'So, so greedy . . .'

'Have you read the letters, Mr Claus?' Wilf tilted his chin.

'Sorry, what was that, young man?'

'I said, have you even read the letters my sister wrote?'

'Ah well, these days I have my trusty team of elves do that for me.'

'So you haven't read them?'

'I don't need to read them because I've seen it all before. Two letters means extra requests and that equals greedy.'

'I don't mean to be rude in any way, sir, but I know you're wrong about my sister. Tizzy isn't spoilt or greedy and I know the letters will prove that.'

'Can I take the letters back?' Tizzy pleaded, her cheeks burning as she tried to stay strong and hold it together. 'You can just miss me out this year, I don't mind.'

The foreman burst out laughing and the other elves joined in.

'Ooh, that's so funny,' the foreman said. 'She wants her letters back!'

'It's certainly unusual.' Santa raised his bushy eyebrows. 'Dig out her letters, return them and then we can all get back to work.'

The mean-looking elf made a face. 'I'll get a printout, if I must.' He tapped away at his keyboard and seconds later the foreman lifted two sheets from the printer.

'One moment – not so fast!' The foreman raised his hand. 'I think it's only fair that we see just how much she did ask for before I hand them over.'

'Oh, that'll be funny,' said the mean-looking elf. 'Go ahead and read them out. Hahaha, I can hardly wait!'

Adjusting his glasses, the foreman peered at the first letter. 'This is it, address: Stargazy Cottage, Duck Street, Mousehole, blah, blah. OK, here we go . . .'

Dear Santa

I hope you are well because I know how important good health is to everyone. I have only one request for Christmas. My mum is ill and I want her to get better. Oh, hold on, make that two – I'd really like a BuzzKidz Game Player, but Mum's health is more important. I hope you and Mrs Claus have a lovely Christmas.

Thank you in advance

Tizzy Biff x

The foreman looked up and his mouth fell open in surprise.

Santa nodded and stroked his beard. 'Read out the other one.'

The mean-looking elf nodded. 'Yeah, that'll show her up – making out she's a goody two-shoes caring about her mum more than herself. I don't believe a word of it!'

The foreman moved on to the next sheet of paper. 'Ashburn House, Elbert Crescent, London. Well now, that's a different address. All rather sneaky, if you ask me.'

Dear Santa

It's me again, Tizzy Biff. I hope you don't mind me writing twice, only I am so worried about my mum. She's so unwell that my brother Wilf and I have been sent all the way to London to stay with our grandma. She's called Gloriana and I'm not sure she wants to be a grandmother. Anyway, Beatrice Bling, who lives next door to Gloriana, has shown me the Marmaduke's website which is full of toys and gifts and she's making me write and ask for what I truly want, and at the same time let you know that we're no longer at home in Cornwall. So here goes:

Please, please, please help my mum get well soon and I'd also like to go home as would Wilf. Oh, and I'd like a BuzzKidz Game Player if that's possible, though I've now asked for three things and maybe that's too much? If so, please make Mum's health my NUMBER ONE request.

Thank you in advance

Tizzy Biff x

PS Happy Christmas to you and Mrs Claus.

The mean-looking elf's face softened and he wiped his eyes.

'Seems like a decent kid,' the foreman said.

The elves nodded in agreement, while Santa blew his nose and cleared his throat. 'My experience may be long,' he said, 'but one can still be surprised.'

Chapter Fourteen

In the middle of the ship was a large open space with a circle of Christmas trees in big pots below a domed skylight.

Looking up, Tizzy and Wilf could see fairy lights twinkling against the dark sky and falling snow outside.

'It's like we're inside a snow dome,' Tizzy smiled.

'Come on through,' Santa said, holding back the branches of one of the Christmas trees to reveal a small clearing where a white-haired woman in a red tracksuit was peddling furiously on an exercise bike.

'Ah, just the excuse I need to stop exercising.' The woman climbed off the bike and wiped her brow. 'Phew, that was long – feels like I've just peddled to Alaska and back!'

'Meet Mrs Claus.' Santa gave his wife a hug.

'Call me Cherie, why don't you?' Mrs Claus said to Tizzy and Wilf. 'Now, if my dear husband could find us some drinks and snacks?'

'Yes, dear.' Santa nodded and went off towards a small log cabin.

'Welcome to the grotto, my lovelies. Come and take a seat.' She gestured towards some tree-trunk stools set around a chunky wooden table. 'We're trying to get fit. Christmas really takes it out of us, you know. We need to feel tip-top. I make Nicholas do an hour a day on the bike. He moans, but he knows it'll help him when the reindeer are tugging. They're so keen to get flying.'

'Make way for some delicious treats.' Santa returned, bearing a tray with a teapot and cups, plates, cakes and biscuits. 'Shall I pour?' He lifted the giant teapot which had holly leaves and red berries on the lid.

Wilf crinkled his nose. 'No tea for me, thank you.'

'But it's chocolate tea and I cannot recommend it enough.' Santa shuffled forward on his stool and lifted the pot, tipping it a fraction until each cup was brimming with chocolate tea.

'It looks like hot chocolate.' Tizzy took a sip. 'It tastes like it too.'

'Ah well, that's the surprise – it's hot chocolate from a teapot, so chocolate tea! Cake or biscuit, anyone?' Santa passed round a cake stand laden with cupcakes and star-shaped cookies covered in red and green icing.

Wilf bit into one of the cookies. 'Ooh, my mouth is fizzing!'

'That's popping candy in the middle,' Santa said with a wink. 'We call them Christmas Crackle Cookies.'

'This reminds me of afternoon tea with the Blings at our grandma's house.' Tizzy thought back to that fateful day when she wrote her second letter to Santa.

Mrs Claus gave a thumbs up. 'I bet you have the best time when you visit your gran?'

'She's not like other grandmas,' Wilf said. 'We have to call her Gloriana.'

'We've only just met her,' Tizzy explained. 'Our mum had to go to hospital so we were sent to stay with Gloriana in London.'

'We'd never been to London before,' Wilf added. 'Mum said it would be an adventure.'

'And it has been an adventure,' Tizzy said, 'but now we're even further away from home and we miss our mum and dad.'

'And the cats,' Wilf added.

'Going home for Christmas would be the best present,' Tizzy said. 'We want to see Mum and Dad and we want Mum to be well.'

Santa put down his cookie. 'You know there's only so much I can do,' he said sadly.

Mrs Claus passed Tizzy a tissue. 'Here you are, lovely, don't you worry now – we'll get you back home, won't we, Nicholas?' She poked Santa in the ribs.

'Yes, dear, whatever you say.'

Wilf shivered at the thought of repeating their long journey. 'Will Seeglo collect us by dog sled?'

'Well, it's nearly Christmas and you need to get home as soon as possible.' Santa stroked his long bushy beard. 'There are other ways that are quicker and easier and toastier.'

'One thing I must ask, did you sign the Official Santa's Secrets Act?' Mrs Claus was clever, and a cautious woman.

Tizzy nodded. 'I did my best curly signature.'

'Me too,' said Wilf.

Mrs Claus smiled. 'It's been a pleasure to have you here, but you must keep quiet about what you've seen on our special ship. We can't have anyone else turning up.'

'We won't say a thing.' Wilf mimed zipping his lip.

'People won't believe you anyway,' Mrs Claus chuckled. 'Right, time to rest before your long journey home.'

She guided them along several corridors and up three flights of stairs to a cosy cabin with bunk beds. 'There you go, my dears. I'll have the elves bring you supper and then get yourselves a good night's sleep.'

Chapter Fifteen

In the early hours, the children woke to hear splashing and what sounded like the clash of swords.

'What was that?' Confused and half asleep, Tizzy peered out through the pane of the cabin porthole. Rubbing her eyes, she stared at the bright green lights snaking across the black sky. 'Wow!'

Wilf joined her at the window. 'It's the northern lights! And look down there!'

Alongside the ship, a gap in the ice had opened to reveal the spiral tusks of two narwhals spinning around each other, tusks clashing.

'The unicorns of the sea.' Tizzy sighed at the magical sight: a swirling green and black sky over the two mysterious creatures playing in the glittering sea – and then they were gone, diving back down into the inky depths.

'That was a bit different to watching the cats back home,' Tizzy said.

'There were two of them,' Wilf smiled.

There was a knock at the door. 'Wakey-wakey!' Mrs Claus called. 'Come on down for breakfast – there are pancakes and waffles.'

Once again, Tizzy and Wilf followed the red route around the vast ship, making their way around a series of winding corridors and down several flights of steps until they arrived at the huge double doors to the dining hall.

Cutlery was clanging and there was the usual chatter.

Wilf pushed open the door and the hundreds of elves seated at the long communal tables looked up, smiled and said good morning.

'Ah, here they are.' Ootah arrived with two plates stacked high with pancakes and waffles and an array of sauces: raspberry, chocolate, maple syrup, caramel and banana. 'I recommend a little of each. It's far too difficult to choose, especially this early in the morning.'

A hush came over the dining hall as everyone tucked in to the feast.

A few minutes later an alarm bell started to ring and a crackly message sounded over the loudspeaker: 'All elves on deck! Repeat, all elves on deck!'

Ootah waved at the children. 'Hurry, it's time to go!'

'But we haven't finished,' Wilf complained.

'Miss this pickup and you miss Christmas back home, kiddo.'

Wilf put down his cutlery, cleared away his plate, and followed Ootah.

Outside on the ice at the bottom gate to the gangway, elves were unloading supplies from the back of two trailers attached to snowmobiles.

'It's Seeglo and Minik,' Ootah explained. 'They're dropping off food for us and taking you home.'

A line of elves had already started carrying boxes up the gangway to the deck.

'All unloaded and ready for the kids,' Cedric said.

Ootah looked sad as they all shook hands.

Tizzy and Wilf, dressed back in their parkas and extra fur coats, said goodbye.

'We'll never forget you,' Tizzy said.

'Hurry!' Seeglo shouted.

'He's getting cold,' Ootah said, 'and we all hate goodbyes.'

'Hold on one moment.' It was a deep booming voice that could belong to only one person. Father Christmas, in his thick red coat trimmed with white fur and big black boots, arrived on deck with a small gift-wrapped package. 'Some of Mrs Claus's Christmas Crackle Cookies to share with your family,' he said. 'Safe journey, my young friends.'

Chapter Sixteen

The crystal walkway glistened with icicles and hundreds of coloured lights. Tizzy and Wilf were tearful as they walked down the gangway and away from the one true grotto.

Outside the gate, Seeglo was waiting. 'You see Sinterklaas?' he asked.

Tizzy and Wilf nodded and smiled.

'Back home?' Seeglo pointed at two snowmobiles. 'We take?'

'Yes, please,' Tizzy nodded.

'Two snowmobiles!' Wilf whooped.

Minik climbed on the first with Wilf on the back and Seeglo took the other with Tizzy and then they covered the many miles over the ice.

Back at the warehouse, the sorting machine was in full swing, sorting thousands of boxes of toys ready for despatch to the various stores worldwide.

With a *clank!* and a *clang!* the machine struggled to cope with its heavy load and the children covered their ears as they hurried past.

'Choose!' Seeglo nodded at the row of wooden doors labelled with the names of shops around the world: Hamleys, the Toy Station, and Mickey's Shop, Florida, to name but a few.

'There's Marmaduke's,' Tizzy noted. 'Gloriana will be waiting for us. She must be worried – we've been ages.'

'She's probably gone.' Wilf made a face. 'Find Bib and Bob's. I want to go home.'

'I want to see Mum,' Tizzy agreed.

Wilf paused by the door to Mickey's Shop. 'Or we could go to Florida?'

Tizzy shot him a sharp look. 'I thought you wanted to go home? I want to see Mum and Dad. I have to know Mum's alright.'

Wilf nodded and they continued to search. 'So many doors,' he huffed. 'They should make them alphabetical.'

Tizzy stopped. 'Maybe it's about the size of shop. I'm guessing it's one of the smaller doors towards the end there.'

She jogged on a little further. 'Look, here it is – I've found it!'

'Okay, let's go!' Wilf pressed the button to open the door.

'Where are Seeglo and Minik? We should say goodbye.'

'They're busy,' Wilf said. 'It's nearly Christmas.'

A siren sounded, the conveyor belt went faster and a horn beeped.

A moment later Seeglo came zipping around the corner in a buggy.

The door marked Bib and Bob's had slid open to reveal a large square lift.

Seeglo held the door back. 'Go now,' he said, and they stepped inside.

Seeglo then loaded a stack of ten or so large brown boxes in front of them until Wilf could no longer see out of the lift. A big strap was passed over the top of the boxes and buckled on either side to a brass handrail that ran around the inside of the lift.

'Press!' Seeglo ordered.

There was one button, labelled Store Room. Tizzy pressed it.

'Bye, Seeglo.' They waved, Wilf's hand only just visible over the top of the boxes. 'Thank you and happy Christmas!'

The doors closed with a *clang!* and the whole lift shot to one side, shook and then whizzed up and up.

Tizzy gasped and grabbed the rail before she fell over.

'Hold on tight!' Wilf said.

The lift slowed down, shot sideways again and then started to drop.

'Whoa, that's fast . . .' Tizzy gripped the rail as tight as she could.

'My ears just popped.' Wilf closed his eyes. 'I feel sick!'

'Are we going up or down?' Tizzy yelled.

Gritting their teeth, they clung on until eventually the lift slowed right down and shuddered to a stop.

'Phew!' Tizzy blew up at her hair. 'Think it's safe to let go now?'

They heard the muffled sound of voices.

'Who's that?' Wilf said.

The doors of the lift clanked open but it was pitch dark beyond.

'Are we there?' Wilf whispered. 'Is this Bib and Bob's?'

They climbed carefully over the pile of boxes, then stepped forward, feeling their way in the dark.

Tizzy found the bottom of some steps on the other side of the room, but her way was blocked by more boxes. 'This must be the way out but we can't get to it.'

'Shush! Did you hear that?' Wilf paused to listen.

It was Bob's voice and he was saying something about fish.

'It's Dad – Bob is talking to Dad! He must be getting a delivery of fish.' Wilf hammered on the door.

'Shush, let me listen.'

There was a tinkle of a bell and a door closed above them.

'He's gone – we've missed him.' Wilf shoved Tizzy. 'You should've let me shout.'

'What if we scare Bob?'

'We have to get out. *Help!*' Wilf yelled.

'Help!' Tizzy joined in. 'Help, we're down here!'

A moment later there were footsteps, the door opened and a few boxes fell out of the storeroom and into the shop.

'Bob, it's us!' Wilf shouted.

'Bib and Bob's, our favourite shop!' Tizzy was grinning but felt herself well up. It was all so familiar: the colourful piles of toys crammed into every nook and cranny of the small shop.

'What was that – who's there?' Bob, wearing a thick woolly sweater with a reindeer on the front, dragged another box into the middle of the shop. 'Is someone there?'

'Bob!' Tizzy called again. 'It's us!'

'What, who's that – who's there? The shop is shut now.' Bob stood on tiptoe to see past the boxes. 'Don't even think about stealing anything, I'll call the police!'

'It's only us, Bob – Tizzy and Wilf.'

'The young Biffs? But you're missing. Everyone is out looking for you. What are you doing down there?'

'It's a long story,' Tizzy said, 'but thank goodness we're here now.'

'Your grandmother was on the news – very upset she was.'

'Really?' Wilf said. 'That doesn't sound like her.'

'The police have been questioning her. People say she didn't look after you and that she's a bad grandma. You've been missing for ages. Where have you been?'

'It must be obvious to you, Bob.' Tizzy turned to point at the lift. 'Oh! Where has it gone?'

'Where's what gone?'

'The lift.'

'Lift?'

'We came by lift with all the boxes of toys.'

'There's no lift in my shop. It's far too small for that.'

'Maybe you call it an elevator?' Wilf suggested.

'It's just back there,' Tizzy stated. 'If you turn on the light we'll show you.'

Bob flicked the light switch and the bare bulb hanging from the ceiling lit up every corner of the basement store room.

'See, there's no lift or elevator or however you want to call it.'

'So what's that wooden door over there?'

'Delivery hatch – allows me to deposit all the boxes of toys straight down here.'

'Can you open it?' Wilf asked. 'I reckon it'll be a lift with buttons.'

'Fine, if you want to see the blue sky.' Bob took his key and unlocked the padlock, opening the doors to the fresh sea air and a bright blue winter sky as a seagull screeched overhead.

'Look, it's just the street, the sky and a seagull.'

Wilf frowned, 'But we came with the boxes.'

'Were you in the van?'

'What van?'

'The postman brought them in his van like he always does.'

Tizzy and Wilf looked at one another.

'We brought them,' Tizzy said. 'They came in the lift with us.'

'There is no lift.' Bob looked away as if he was avoiding eye contact. 'Why would a small shop like this need a lift?'

'Oh, I get it.' Tizzy rolled her eyes. 'It's a secret, because everything to do with Father Christmas has to be secret or his job would become too difficult. You've signed the Official Santa's Secrets Act.'

Bob's cat, Bib, came down the steps and wound himself round Bob's legs.

'He wants feeding. I got some fantastic fish from your dad. Right, I'd better hurry up.' Bob picked up the phone and dialled. 'They're here, though goodness knows how. Yes, yes, safe and sound.'

Chapter Seventeen

The TV reporter pushed a microphone in Tizzy's face.

'So how did you find your way back home to Cornwall?'

'We got a lift,' Tizzy said.

'Someone drove you the whole way here?'

'It was very fast,' Wilf said.

'But it took a few days – did you stop along the way?'

Tizzy nodded. 'Yes, we did.'

'We wanted to visit Santa's Grotto,' Wilf said.

'Santa's Grotto?' The TV reporter raised her eyebrows and smiled. 'And did you manage to see Santa?'

Tizzy sighed. She knew this woman wasn't taking them seriously, but then again perhaps it was better this way.

'We can't really say,' Tizzy said. 'We signed the Official Santa's Secrets Act.'

The woman's shoulders shook and her microphone wobbled as she tried not to laugh. 'Well, as we all know, there are only two days to go until Christmas and what better news for you and your family than to have you safely back home – however you got here.'

The TV cameraman shifted his focus to Gloriana, who was standing nearby in a long pea-green coat, hat and shiny boots.

'Grandma Biff, you must be relieved to have your

grandchildren safely home?' The reporter thrust her microphone towards Gloriana.

'It's Gloriana Biff, thank you,' she snapped.

'Gloriana Biff, your grandchildren went missing while under your care. How are you feeling after their safe return?'

Gloriana raised her chin. 'I'm glad they're back where they belong,' she said crisply.

'She means back here with Mum and Dad,' Wilf whispered, 'and no longer getting in the way of her beauty treatments and holidays.'

'That's fine by me,' Tizzy said.

Gloriana put her stiff arms around Tizzy and Wilf and smiled for the cameras as dozens of flashes went off, making Tizzy and Wilf blink, while Gloriana turned her head to the left a little, making sure the photographers got her best side.

Chapter Eighteen

The cats were back behind Stargazy Cottage.

Delicious wafts from Dad's cooking had seeped through the cracks around the kitchen door and window. Some cats mewed or paced up and down as they waited, while greedier cats both mewed *and* paced *and* licked their lips. A screech of seagulls whirled above the chimney pots, ready to dive on any last scraps.

It was Tom Bawcock's Eve, two nights before Christmas – a time to celebrate the long-ago fisherman who went out in a storm to bring back enough fish to save the village from famine.

'This pie's a *winner!*' said Dad, pulling his steaming dish from the oven.

Wilf nodded. 'Fourteen fish. That's a good number.'

'Yes, but what about my *pie*?' Dad stood back to gaze at his thick-crusted creation. It was the usual mix of fish, egg and potato and the fourteen fish heads poking out looked like they were bobbing along in an eggy potato ocean.

'It makes me think of the narwhals popping through the cracks in the ice,' Wilf said.

'*Shush!*' hissed Tizzy, giving Wilf a hard stare.

Gloriana tutted. 'What's all this rubbish about narwhals? Children who tell silly stories should be sent to their rooms without supper.'

'There are narwhals in Wilf's book about the Arctic,' Tizzy explained.

Wilf nodded, 'Yes, that's right – there's a photo of them popping their heads up out of the sea.'

Mum smiled as she ruffled Wilf's hair. 'My ducklings have had an enormous adventure. All the way from Duck Street to London.' With tears in her eyes, she said, 'I'm so happy to have you both home for Christmas.'

Dad put his arm round Gloriana's stiff shoulders. 'It's good to have you here as well after all this time. Grannies are important!' He grinned. 'Now you've finally visited and can see life down here in Cornwall isn't so bad, won't you stay for Christmas?'

Gloriana's mouth went twisty as if there was something she needed to spit out. 'Thank you for the invite, but I don't think so. I'm craving sunshine, beaches and a luxury cruise.'

Wilf perked up. 'What sort of cruise ship?'

Gloriana rolled her eyes. 'I don't care what sort of cruise ship it is so long as it has fancy food and people like me.'

'People like you?' Wilf was confused.

'Smart people in smart clothes.'

Tizzy made a face.

'Well, you'll spend tonight with us at least?' Dad asked.

'You can see the harbour lights and the lantern parade,' Tizzy said.

They all wrapped up in their warm winter coats with hats and scarves.

'No need to brush your hair,' Tizzy whispered.

Wilf pulled his bobble hat down low over his ears.

'Good idea,' Mum smiled and did the same, pulling her woolly hat low, hiding her hair which had got thinner lately. 'Ready?' Mum took some paper lanterns out of the cupboard and gave one each to Tizzy and Wilf. 'I made these for you.'

'Narwhals!' Their eyes lit up at the sight of the carefully

crafted lanterns.

'I looked at the photo in your book on the Arctic,' Mum winked.

Outside, the streets of Mousehole were bright with coloured lights as Dad proudly delivered his stargazy pie to the Star Inn for the annual pie contest.

Tizzy and Wilf held their bobbing narwhals up high as the family joined the long stream of villagers and visitors winding slowly through the twisting streets of Mousehole.

Gloriana's face cracked a little.

Wilf nudged Tizzy. 'I think she's smiling.'

'Are you OK, Gloriana?' Tizzy asked.

'It's all rather sweet.' Gloriana's eyes looked a little misty.

Tizzy took her grandma's hand. 'I told you Mousehole is magical at Christmas.'

The harbour lights were shining bright. A neon whale floated out on the water among the bobbing boats, while along the harbour wall sat sleighs, twinkling stars, Christmas trees, Christmas puds and stripy stockings.

At the door to Bib and Bob's Toyshop stood Bob with his cat Bib in his arms. 'Happy Christmas to the Biffs!' he cried as they passed.

The parade wormed its way through every street and then back to the Star Inn – the famous one and only pub by the harbour. A giant stargazy pie in flashing lights flickered a welcome from the harbour wall outside.

It was time for the results of the annual stargazy pie contest.

'This is it.' Wilf gave Dad the thumbs up. 'Good luck!'

'This has got to be my year.' Dad held his breath.

The landlady came out to make the announcement. 'What brilliant pies! It has been *so* hard to choose a winner, but here goes. The prize for this year's *best*, most *incredible* pie goes to . . . JEROME BRIGGS!'

The crowd whooped while Tizzy and Wilf patted their dad on the back.

'There's always next year,' Tizzy said.

'What were they thinking?' Wilf shook his head. 'The winning pie has twenty-five fish. *Twenty-five!* That's a horrid number!'

Dad's pie had been beaten by an even bigger, even better stargazy pie.

'Never mind,' Dad said, collecting his pie. 'At least I can share it with the cats.'

'What a strange-looking thing the stargazy is.' Gloriana wrinkled her nose. 'Do you really eat that?'

Mum laughed. 'It tastes better than it looks.'

'I dare you to try it.' Tizzy nudged her grandma.

'I think I'll just have some toast and marmalade until I join the luxury cruise tomorrow.'

'You're really leaving tomorrow?' Dad looked surprised. 'You'll miss out on Christmas in Cornwall with your family.

Most grandmas love Christmas with their families.'

'It's that word again.' Gloriana winced. 'Have you not realised? I'm *not* like most grandmas.'

'And you'll miss out on the Christmas Crackle Cookies,' Wilf said.

'Christmas Crackle Cookies – what on earth are they?'

'We're not allowed to say.' Wilf raised his chin.

Tizzy nodded. 'Santa wouldn't like it and neither would Mrs Claus.'

Raising their narwhal lanterns, Tizzy and Wilf led the way home, followed by a grumbling Gloriana, a tired but happy Mum, Dad with his stargazy pie – and then a long line of cats happily following the tasty smell of Dad's cooking all the way home to Stargazy Cottage, Duck Street, Mousehole, Cornwall, near the bottom left-hand corner of England.

Acknowledgements

A big thank you to my editor and friend Monica Byles whose commitment and sharp-eyed brilliance makes her a joy to work with.

Thanks to my friends and family, especially Bijou and Zanzi for their tips on Photoshop, Morgan, Julia, Mum and Dad, and my partner Daryl for their love and support.

Jacqui Hazell

Jacqui Hazell is the author of Horace Fox in the City. She writes award-winning fiction for children, young adults and adults (writing as Jaq Hazell). She lives in London with her family and her little dog Basil. You may also spot Jacqui as an extra in TV shows and films!

To find out more about Jacqui's books and to download a free picture of Horace Fox visit jacquihazell.com

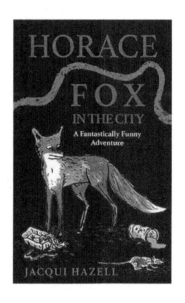

Horace Fox is being followed.
Deadly hit-snake Zigzag McVitie is after him.
Horace has been left a swish den in London but
evil Badger Burnhard wants it.

Can Horace avoid the snake, beat the badger,
and claim the den in time?
And will his stomach ever stop rumbling?

HORACE FOX IN THE CITY

'Children will love following Horace's brave journey,' *NB Magazine*

'Danger, mystery, and intrigue, this was a fun read' *Dark Raven Reviews*

'It's a delightful read with lovely illustrations' *Fox N The City*

A fantastic fast-paced adventure from an award-winning author.

Perfect for children aged 6-11 and for fox fans everywhere!

For Young Adult Readers

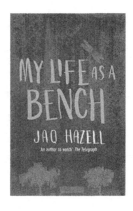

Winner of the International Rubery Book of the
Year Award
Winner of the Carousel Aware Prize Best Young
Adult Book

'Moving and unforgettable' *Rubery Book Award*
'Unique . . . deep and intriguing' *Times of India*
'Delightful, honest and humorous' *School
Library Journal*

If you've enjoyed Elf Road, please leave a
review on Amazon & Goodreads

Thanks for reading!

Printed in Great Britain
by Amazon